Praise for N.J. Walters The Way Home

4.0! "The Way Home is a book about just that. It's about knowing what is home to you and not settling for anything less....If you are looking for a light, heart felt romance to wile away some lazy hours then I reckon you will enjoy the folks of Jamesville."
~Janet Davies, Once Upon A Romance Review

4 Cups "...a touching story that reaches out to the reader...blends a story with great dialogue and wonderful magnetism that brings out the in-depth emotions of the couple in this charming installment."
~Cherokee, Coffee Time Romance

"N.J. Walters has written a lovely and emotional story and if you like romance, you will love reading *The Way Home*. This is a relaxing story to just sit down with and enjoy."
~Annick, Euro-Reviews

The Way Home

By N. J. Walters

A Samhain Publishing, Ltd. publication.

Samhain Publishing, Ltd.
2932 Ross Clark Circle, #384
Dothan, AL 36301

The Way Home
Copyright © 2006 by N. J. Walters
Cover by Scott Carpenter
Print ISBN: 1-59998-252-8
Digital ISBN: 1-59998-078-9
www.samhainpublishing.com

First Samhain Publishing, Ltd. electronic publication: July 2006
First Samhain Publishing, Ltd. print publication: October 2006

Dedication

Thank you to Crissy and Ansley for loving this book enough to accept it for publication. Thank you to my wonderful editor, Jessica Bimberg for all her hard work in making this story even better.

As always, thank you to my wonderful husband. Without your support this book would never have been written.

Chapter One

"So, will you marry me?"

Rebecca Gentry sat at her pine kitchen table and blinked at the man she loved, not quite certain she had heard him correctly. In all her twenty-five years, when she had dared to imagine such a proposal, it had come nowhere close to this. She had envisioned wildflowers, a declaration of love and a man down on one knee, holding her hand tight in his. Never had she imagined a plainspoken business proposition.

She knew she was sitting there with her mouth open. She also knew he expected her to say something. But the plain fact was she couldn't think of anything to say.

"You want me to marry you?" Rebecca questioned slowly, still not certain she had heard him right.

"Yes."

Jake Tanner was a good-looking man, she thought as she continued to stare at him. Not classically good-looking, but handsome in a rugged way. She never tired of looking at his weatherworn face.

His green eyes looked hard as emeralds and the deep creases radiating from their corners only added to the image of strength. His black hair was swept away from his face in a careless manner and hung down to his shoulders in the back. It always looked as if he'd just pushed it out of his way. She wanted to run her hands through his hair and she found herself clasping her hands in her lap, as she frequently did around him, to keep herself from reaching out to touch it.

He stood a shade under six feet tall, which was head and shoulders over her, as she was half an inch over five feet. His shoulders were broad and solid from years of hard physical labor on his farm and that made him look even larger than he actually was.

Rebecca stared straight into his eyes, hoping to gain a clue into what had prompted this strange proposal. "Why?"

Jake leaned forward in his chair and laid both hands flat on the table. "I need a wife, Rebecca, not some silly woman who thinks she's in love one day and gone the next. I respect you. Heck, I really like you. We've been friends for seven years. I know you're a hard worker, you're loyal, and you don't run away when things get tough. You've lived here all your life and you seem happy here. I think we could make a go of a marriage."

Rebecca instantly picked up on the one point that mattered. "What do you mean, you *need* a wife?"

Jake sighed deeply and sat back in his chair, making it creak slightly as it adjusted to his weight. Absently, he thrust a hand through his hair, tilting back his head as his eyes searched the ceiling as if somehow the right words were written there. "You know I just got back today from my brother's and sister-in-law's funeral."

She instantly leaned across the table and laid her hand on his strong, denim-clad forearm, squeezing it gently. She wished there was some way she could help alleviate his sorrow. "I know, and I'm sorry about Hank and his wife. I know you weren't close, but it's still got to be hard, maybe even harder because of that."

"You got that right." He pulled his gaze from the ceiling and gave her a mocking little smile. "Hank couldn't wait to scrape the dirt from his boots and get away from the farm as soon as he was old enough. All he wanted was the city life and I don't blame him for that. Farming isn't for everyone. But no, we were never close."

Reaching into his shirt pocket, he withdrew a small white envelope, and held it out to her. She accepted it tentatively, peered inside, and withdrew a picture of a small family. A dark-haired man stood behind a lovely looking blond woman who held a wide-eyed little girl on her lap. Rebecca found herself captivated by the child, a green-eyed imp with black hair, who looked enough like Jake to be his own daughter.

"That was taken a few months ago." He reached over and plucked the picture from her fingers. "I got it in my Christmas card this year. That's Hank, his wife Celine, and their daughter Casey."

"They were a beautiful family." Her heart went out to Jake. She handed him the envelope and watched as he carefully replaced the picture and tucked it back in his pocket.

"Casey was at home with a babysitter when Hank and Celine were in the car accident. From what I could gather, they went away a lot of weekends without her." He shook his head in disgust. "Anyhow, Hank named me her legal guardian, but I would have taken her anyway because family is family."

He took a deep breath and voiced his fears. "It doesn't matter that I've never seen her in person until a few days ago. I'm going to bring her home with me. But, Rebecca, I don't think I can raise a four-year-old girl on my own."

Rebecca nodded. "That's why you suddenly need a wife." It was more of a statement than a question, but Jake confirmed it anyway.

He sighed and his normally hard eyes softened. "She's quiet and withdrawn, and she seems confused by everything. She cried and slept almost all the time I was with her. Her babysitter agreed to stay with her for a week while I tried to arrange things here." He ran his hand through his hair again, his agitation plain.

"I could hire a housekeeper, but I think she needs stability right now more than anything else. Besides, I'm not getting any younger myself, and I'd like to have some kids of my own." He glanced at her, giving her a quick smile. "I don't think anyone else would have me, I'm stubborn and set in my ways."

"But this is very sudden, Jake. You never seemed interested in me, romantically that is."

He sat quietly for a minute, as if picking and choosing his words carefully. "I like you more than I do any other woman. You're a good friend and companion. Physically, I find you very attractive, but I admit if this hadn't come up I probably wouldn't be asking you to marry me."

"I see," she answered in a soft voice as she looked quickly into her lap. She knew he was watching her, and hoped to hide the pain that his words caused her.

"Rebecca, you know I'll always be honest with you." He reached out and took her hand in his larger, darker one. "I thought about it a lot the last few days. I'm alone now except for Casey and it made me think about a family of my own, something I haven't done in years. I'm a plainspoken man, not a romantic one. I don't believe in foolish romantics, but I do believe in friendship and commitment. There isn't another woman I would ask what I'm asking you. I think we could have a good marriage."

She stared at their joined hands, one large and callused, the other small and soft. "I just don't know. It's all so sudden."

"I know it is, but I don't have much time to wait. I've got to leave in a couple days to drive back to get Casey. I've got some legal things to get through here and with Hank's lawyers in New York. That barely leaves enough time to take care of the legalities of a wedding and get a prenuptial agreement drawn up."

Rebecca was stunned by the hard, business-like attitude, even though she had expected it from him. "You want a prenuptial agreement?"

He squeezed her hand reassuringly. "I expect our marriage to work and I know you'd never try to take the farm if it didn't. But legally you'd be entitled to part of it and I'm not taking any chances with the legal system. It's simpler this way and don't worry, I'll have a clause written in to make sure you're taken care of if something does happen and you decide you want a divorce someday."

"You almost sound as if you expect I'd change my mind." Despite her efforts, she was unable to keep the hurt from her voice.

The muscles in Jake's jaw hardened, and his words were bitter. "Farm life is hard on a woman and I've yet to meet one who would stick it out."

His expression relaxed a bit as he looked across the table at her. "I trust you to stay more than I would any other woman. I wouldn't be asking you to marry me otherwise. So, what do you say?"

Her heart pounded and she rubbed her hand against her chest in a futile attempt to make it stop. "Jake, I can't answer right now. I have so much to think about. Please, give me some time."

"It would be easier if you could answer me now, but I guess I have taken you off guard." Jake stood up and hauled on his fleece-lined jacket. "I'd give you more time if I had it, but I have to know by the morning. If you're not going to marry me I have to try and hire a housekeeper in the next two days."

"Tomorrow morning." She had a sinking feeling that her well-ordered life was toppling out of control.

She watched him as he made his way over to the door of her apartment. He opened it, but turned back for one last look. "Tomorrow, Rebecca." He walked out the door and closed it quietly behind him.

Rebecca slumped in her chair and stared at the closed door as she listened to his boots pound down the outside stairs. She didn't know how long she sat there, but it was long past dark before she made herself get up, lock the door, and drag herself to bed.

Chapter Two

Several hours later, she lay in bed with her eyes wide open, staring at her bedroom ceiling. Her mind kept turning in circles. Yes, she loved Jake. She had loved him in her own quiet way for years, but could she marry him and legally bind herself to a man who admittedly didn't love her?

If she was honest with herself, and she always tried to be, she was already bound to him. Her heart and all her love belonged to the big, somber man who didn't believe in love. If she married him at least she would be able to give him her love in tangible ways, even if she could never tell him that she loved him.

They were both alone in the world. Would it be so wrong to marry him if she loved him? She would be his wife and companion and the mother of his children. She wanted children of her own to love and she knew she would love them even more if Jake were their father. Actually, she couldn't imagine another man she would consider having children with.

Jake was steadfast and loyal. The first to come and help during a crisis, and the last one to leave. Many families in the community owed him their thanks, but he shied away from any signs of gratitude. She knew at least five people in the community who owed their lives to the fact that he was a volunteer firefighter.

Growing up in the small community, she had heard all the rumors about Jake's mother. People still gossiped about the fact that Mrs. Tanner had left town the same afternoon that her husband was buried. When Jake got older and started dating, but never settled down, townsfolk speculated that his mother's actions might have tainted the whole idea of marriage for her son. The older women gossiped in the beauty shop about the fact his mother had hated the farm and, as a result, Jake didn't trust women. The whispers became even louder as the dating became less frequent and he started keeping to himself more.

But, her heart cried, what if he never comes to love me? What happens if someday he meets someone he can love? He would never leave her and she would have to live with that knowledge, and quite simply, it would destroy her.

Unable to stay in bed any longer, she threw back the covers and padded barefoot out into the living room of her apartment. She always felt a thrill when she entered the living room of her small two-bedroom apartment. It was here that she had fulfilled a lifelong dream.

The room held Rebecca's Sewing Studio. It had several shelves along one wall, which held materials and sewing notions, while a long cutting table stretched in front of them. Two sewing machines were set up in front of the window. One was an industrial grade machine for heavy material, such as leather and canvas, and the other—a smaller yet complex one—had helped her created more wedding and prom dresses than she could count.

Material adorned with bright, cheerful sunflowers covered a screen that graced one corner of the room. It not only added color but also provided the necessary dressing room area. Several comfortable chairs were positioned around a small coffee table and plants vied for space in huge planters strategically placed on the gleaming hardwood floor. The effect was one of an airy, open space, and the profusion of ivy and leafy green plants mixed well with the yellow and green colors that dominated the room.

She'd come a long way since finishing high school here in Jamesville. Her father had remarried and moved to Arizona with his new wife as soon as Rebecca had graduated. They had never been close, and now they exchanged cards at birthdays and Christmas. Rebecca had gotten a job as a cashier at Greer's Grocery and Gas Bar, and Mr. Greer had rented her one of the apartments above the store for a very reasonable rent.

She had sewn her own clothing, as money had always been tight. Her father had been a migratory farm worker in the warm months and a laborer in the winter. Work had been uncertain, at best. As a result, she had grown up with little but the basics.

Still, it hadn't been such a bad life, merely a lonely one. Her father had been gone a lot, and she had grown up on her own after her mother had left when she was five. Simply thinking about it made her heart ache for little Casey Tanner. She knew what it was like to feel the lack of a mother. No one to bake treats and greet you after school with a smile. No one to kiss your hurts away. No one to confide your childish dreams to. No one to teach you about clothing, boys and all those other important adolescent things. No matter how other people tried to make up for it, no one could replace a mother's love, but she would try and fill that gap in Casey's life.

Her business had started out as a way for her to earn some extra money. Making a custom set of drapes for a neighbor, hemming a pair of pants for a friend, and sewing costumes for a school pageant seemed to fill her spare time. Before she knew it she was bringing in as much money at her sewing as she was working as a cashier.

She was also putting in fourteen-hour days and she knew it had to stop. She had approached Mr. Greer about setting up her sewing studio in her apartment. While he had been sorry to see her leave the store, he had supported her idea of locating the studio in her home.

The arrangement was actually beneficial to both of them. It made a convenient stop for women who wanted some sewing done. They could easily drop into her studio while they were there to pick up groceries or get some gas. They got all their errands run in one convenient stop. Some women had even started to do more shopping at Greer's because they had to run up to her sewing shop. Besides which, she still filled in every now and then when they were short-handed in the grocery store. All in all, she had been very pleased with her life.

Oh, she was lonely at times. Her job kept her busy and she didn't date at all. She had been what is commonly referred to as a "late bloomer." She had always been small for her age and had stopped growing completely when she had reached the great height of five feet and one-half inch. Add to that a slight build, short brown hair, and pale blue eyes and she had looked like a child until she'd turned eighteen. By then, she'd had enough of a bosom to notice. Not much, but enough for Peter Finch to ask her to the senior prom.

She remembered her prom for two reasons. Not because it was such a wonderful night to remember, but because it was the most traumatic night of her life. It was the night of her first date and the night that she fell in love.

She had been so excited to be going to the prom that she had sewn a new dress. It was a three-quarter length, baby blue dress with a modest neckline and lacy trim. Money she couldn't afford to spend had been spent on a tiny bottle of lavender perfume and a pale pink lipstick. Everything was perfect.

Peter had looked incredibly handsome in his charcoal gray suit. His blonde hair and blue eyes made him popular with the girls—that and the fact he played on the football team. She had repeatedly pinched herself all night long just to make sure she wasn't dreaming. She had been the envy of many of the girls at school. When Peter had pulled his truck to a stop on the side of the road on the way home, she was sure he was going to steal a kiss. Her very first kiss. Her pink-tinted lips had pursed in anticipation.

What she had gotten was more than a kiss. He had grabbed her and smashed his lips down on hers as his hands had started pulling down the top of her dress. Rebecca had frozen with panic. When his hand had touched her bare skin, she'd started to fight and to scream. Peter had gotten angry with her and started yelling that she owed him since he had asked her to the prom. After all, everyone knew she didn't get asked out. She should show him some appreciation for tonight.

She'd shown him appreciation all right. She'd bit him when he tried to thrust his tongue in her mouth. She was still fighting and kicking as he pulled back his hand to hit her.

"What the hell is going on here?" A male voice roared as Peter's weight was suddenly pulled off her.

She heard the sound of angry male voices and the unmistakable sound of flesh meeting flesh. Suddenly, the door on her side of the truck had been yanked open. She had pulled her shredded dress up over her breasts as best she could, but there was little she could do to disguise the fact that it had been ripped off of her. Tears streamed down her face as she sobbed in fear and pain.

"It's okay, little one, it's okay."

Strong arms surrounded her as a low male voice continued to comfort her. Her head jerked up and she came face to face with Jake Tanner. He saw the way she was holding her dress and his face grew hard. His eyes seem to glow with anger.

She pulled back, almost afraid of him, but his voice had soothed her. Before she knew it, his jacket was wrapped around her and she was in his arms. He stopped only long enough to issue a warning to the younger man who was only now picking himself up off the ground in front of the truck.

"You come near this little girl again and you'll answer to me. Do you understand?" Jake glared at the boy in front of him, and his voice held a promise of retribution.

"Yessir," Peter had answered, jumped in his truck and fled.

When she was safely tucked in the passenger seat of Jake's truck, he turned to her. "Are you all right? Do you want me to take you to the hospital?"

She'd lowered her head and shaken it, filled with absolute misery. "I want to go home." Her voice trembled and her teeth chattered as she spoke. Her small body shook with the remnants of her fear. She watched as his hands clenched the steering wheel so tight that his knuckles were white. He seemed as if he might say something more, but she turned away before he could speak, not ready to answer any questions. A softly spoken swear word had singed her ears, but he put the truck in gear and drove.

Jake had taken her home. When he had discovered her father was not there, he had come inside with her. He sent her to take a hot shower, and by the time she came down the stairs, tightly wrapped in her ankle-length flannel gown and robe, he had a cup of tea waiting for her. He had sat down with her and, between sips of too sweet tea, made her talk until she had told him everything.

Her one and only date had been a disaster, but he never criticized or implied in any way that it was her fault. He dried her eyes for her and held her when she shook. Never in her entire life had anyone cared for her like this. In that moment, as she looked into his deep green eyes, she had fallen in love.

It had been puppy love to be sure, but as the months went by and Rebecca moved out on her own, Jake had checked in on her from time to time. They ate together sometimes. She baked him pies and he fixed her plumbing, but she had understood from the beginning that he was a solitary man. He rarely talked about himself and his eyes seemed to carry the remnants of an old pain. As the years went by puppy love had blossomed into a woman's deep abiding love.

Sighing, she shook her thoughts away from the past. She continued to stare out the living room window, looking into the dark night sky for answers that weren't there. The street was empty of cars and people, and there was no movement in the empty lot across from her. She rubbed her hands up and down her arms trying to warm herself as she brought her musings back to the present. Therein lay her problem. She loved Jake. Really, truly loved him. And time had proven that her love was not going to go away any time soon. Didn't she owe it to herself to grab this chance at happiness?

If she married Jake, she would see him everyday for the rest of her life. She would go to bed with him each night and wake up with him each morning. There would be holidays and birthdays spent together, and maybe if they were blessed, there would be children as well.

Shivering, as the chill of the night seeped into her bones, she padded back to her small bedroom and huddled under the handmade quilts. She knew she loved Jake and she felt she could love and understand little Casey as well. Deep in her heart, she knew she had already made her decision. There really was no other choice for her but to marry Jake and give him all of her love. And maybe, if she was lucky, someday she could teach him to love her too.

Chapter Three

"I now pronounce you man and wife." Judge Manning closed the book in his hands with a thump. They both continued to stare at him.

"You may kiss the bride," the judge encouraged when neither one of the couple standing in front of him seemed inclined to move.

Jake started at the judge's words and glanced down at the woman who stood next to him. Pale, but composed, she looked petite and delicate standing beside him. Her short brown hair left her nape bare, giving her an almost vulnerable appearance.

As he lowered his lips to hers, her blue eyes slowly closed, causing her light brown lashes to fan across her high cheekbones. He brushed her mouth with his, marveling at the softness of her rosy lips. He drew back, raising his head again. Her cheeks were flushed a light shade of pink.

That slight contact shook him to the core, but he quickly pushed the feeling aside and turned to the man standing patiently in front of them.

"Thanks, Judge." Jake extended his hand to the smiling man. Judge Manning, with his sharp blue eyes, white hair, and bushy white beard, might resemble Santa Claus, but Jake knew he had a reputation for being both shrewd and discreet. There would be no questions about the suddenness of this marriage and no gossip either about the prenuptial agreement they had signed, along with the other necessary papers, in his presence before the ceremony. "We appreciate you fitting us in on such short notice."

"No problem at all, my boy," the older man assured as he shook Jake's proffered hand. "Weddings are one of the few nicer aspects of my job, but I do have to get to court now if you'll excuse me." He stopped long enough to give Rebecca's hand a gentle squeeze, and then he was gone.

"Come on, honey, and I'll buy you some breakfast." Jake quickly ushered Rebecca into her coat and out of the judge's chambers. They walked in silence down the almost empty corridor and through the front door of the courthouse. With one hand on the small of her back, he used his free hand to unbutton the tight collar of his best dress shirt. He'd donned it, a pair of fresh jeans and a sport coat when he'd dressed this morning. He'd thought it best to dress up a little for the judge's chambers.

As he tucked Rebecca into the front seat of his truck, he was glad he'd thought to clear the junk out of the front seat yesterday. He had the door closed before it occurred to him that she hadn't spoken a word since the brief ceremony had ended.

Hurrying around the front of his black pickup truck, he absently noted the dusty white of the winter road salt. He made a mental not to run it through the car wash. Once settled behind the wheel, he turned to face the woman who was now his wife. "Are you all right, Rebecca?" She was so quiet and unmoving in the seat next to him, it was starting to worry him.

"I'm fine, I think." She offered him a weak smile. "I can hardly believe we're married is all. It seems like a dream."

He stared at her for a long moment, trying to sense her mood. When she said nothing else, he decided to take her at her word. He started the truck and headed the short distance down the road to Jessie's Diner. Some breakfast and coffee would help settle them both.

But it was no dream, Rebecca thought as she huddled in the front seat of the truck. Her hands clutched her purse tight. She desperately needed something to anchor her. Her fingers were digging into the leather so hard, she knew it would have permanent marks on it. The plain gold band on her left hand felt heavy and strange. She had just married Jake Tanner, the man of her dreams, and none of it felt real. She had hardly seen him in the two days since she had accepted his proposal. They had gone to apply for the license together, but other than that she hadn't laid eyes on him until he picked her up this morning.

She'd been nervously applying her lipstick when she'd heard the pounding on her front door. Taking one last look at her appearance in the bedroom mirror, she figured she looked as good as she could on such short notice. She'd dressed in her Sunday best, a long-sleeved, royal blue dress with a full skirt that fell to just below her knees. The bodice was fitted and had six pearl buttons down the front. She barely had time to make sure the collar was lying straight before the pounding started again.

"Rebecca!" She could hear him shouting as she rushed to the apartment door and pulled it open. "We're gonna be late if we don't hurry. The judge is fitting us in before court."

He'd barely given her time to tug on her coat, grab her purse, and lock the door before he'd hurried her down the stairs and into his truck. And now she was back in his truck again. Only this time they were married.

"What are we doing here?" Rebecca was shaken out of her musings when she realized the truck was no longer moving.

Jake turned and grinned sheepishly at her. "I don't know about you, but I didn't eat a thing this morning. I was too nervous about getting married."

The fact that he, too, had been nervous helped her feel a little more confident. After all, this was Jake. She had known him forever, and they had always been comfortable in each other's company. She offered him a warm smile. "Me too. But I could sure go for some eggs and bacon now. I'm starving."

He got out of the truck and came around to her door, taking her hand in his as she stepped down out of the truck. It was a cold morning, even for February, and a light snow was falling as they hurried up the walkway and into Jessie's Diner.

The bell over the door tinkled merrily as they stepped inside the welcoming heat. They brushed the flakes from their hair and stamped the slush from their boots before making their way to the far end of the room where they settled into an empty booth.

Jessie's was an old fashioned diner. The tables were covered with red checked cloths that matched the curtains at the windows. The booth seats and the chairs were upholstered in red vinyl and creaked and groaned when you sat on them. The napkins were in a metal dispenser, at each table and booth, alongside the salt, pepper, ketchup and vinegar bottles. There were eight booths running along the window side of the diner, offering some privacy as well as a view of Main Street. There were also eight tables, which sat four people at each, as well as a dozen stools in front of the counter for anyone who wished to sit there. The food was simple, but it was abundant and delicious.

Jessie herself bustled up to the table to take their order. She was a smart-looking woman in her early forties, whose red hair was now beginning to be streaked with gray. Her figure was still trim and her blue eyes twinkled with humor, as if she was privy to some joke that the rest of the world was not. She had been widowed young and had never remarried, but she and her diner had become a Jamesville institution.

"Good morning, you two." Jessie turned their coffee cups right side up and poured two cups of steaming hot coffee. "I'm surprised to see you at this time of the day, Rebecca. It's not like you not to be hard at work by now."

Rebecca smiled as the other woman bustled about. Jessie was one of her favorite people, often feeding her sandwiches and pie when she was growing up. Somehow, Jessie had always sensed when there had been nothing to eat at home and had managed to make Rebecca think she was doing her a favor by eating the last piece of pie before it went stale or a sandwich someone had ordered and supposedly forgotten. She was the closest thing Rebecca had to a mother figure, so she spoke without hesitation.

"It's a special occasion this morning, Jessie. Jake and I just got married." Rebecca waited to see how she would react to the sudden announcement.

The coffeepot hit the table with a clunk and Jessie opened her mouth and closed it again, seemingly at a loss for words. She recovered quickly, bending down and wrapping Rebecca in a tight hug. "Congratulations." Releasing Rebecca, Jessie turned and pinned Jake with a stern stare. "I hope you know how lucky you are to get her. You treat her right, you hear."

"I hear, Jessie, and thanks." Uncomfortable with the attention, he picked up his menu and studied the breakfast specials.

Rebecca could see the unasked questions in Jessie's eyes. Why so sudden? Why hadn't Rebecca told anyone? Why had they gotten married on a weekday morning?

Wanting to head off any of Jessie's questions, she spoke quickly. She didn't want the other woman digging into the reasons behind the quick wedding. "Thanks, Jessie. Be sure and tell Shannon for me, will you?" Shannon, Jessie's niece, worked at the diner. Rebecca had known her all her life and liked the younger woman.

Jessie's smile faltered for a moment. Rebecca knew the other woman was worried about her, but also knew that she wouldn't pry. Rebecca placed a hand over her stomach to try and settle the butterflies fluttering around inside. It was going to be hard to tell everyone about the wedding and still keep the real reasons behind it a secret.

"I'll tell her when I hear from her. She got herself married last week and moved to Portland with her new husband." Jessie smiled, but it didn't quite reach her eyes. "Now, what would you like for breakfast? It's on the house."

They placed their order and ate quietly when it was served. At least Jake ate, shoveling down his food as she picked at hers. That was another thing that Rebecca liked about being with Jake. She didn't always have to have something to talk about. Their silences were the comfortable kind and neither of them felt the need to make conversation while they ate.

Rebecca turned the plain gold band on her left hand around and around as she stared at it. Jake's larger, rougher hand suddenly covered hers, making her glance up at him.

"Let's go to your place so we can be alone." Plunking down his coffee cup, he released her hand and slid out of the booth.

"All right." She scooted out of her seat and pulled on her coat. She was more than ready to be alone with Jake. This was their wedding day after all.

Jessie refused to let them pay for breakfast, reminding them that it was her wedding gift to them. Rebecca barely had time to thank Jessie and ask her to pass on their congratulations to Shannon on her wedding before Jake was hustling her out the door.

Chapter Four

The ride to her apartment was short and in no time at all they were back at her place. Jake was sitting at the small table in the corner of her little blue and white kitchen when she returned from freshening up, his elbows resting on the table, his eyes serious. Nervously, she straightened the dishtowel hanging on the stove handle, picked up the dishcloth and wiped down the already immaculate counter. As Jake continued to stare at her, she folded the cloth, laid it on the table and perched on the edge of a chair. "Well, here we are again." She tried to smile.

The serious expression on his face didn't change and she felt her smile falter. "What's wrong, Jake?"

Reaching into his pocket, he removed a set of keys and laid them on the table. "Here's the keys to the house. I shouldn't be gone for more then a week, maybe less."

"You're leaving?" Rebecca noticed she was strangling the poor dishcloth that she'd laid on the table and forced herself to release it.

"Yeah, I've got my bag packed and in the truck. If I leave now I should be back with Casey in five or six days. I'll only be gone as long as it takes to get her stuff packed up and their apartment cleared out. I'm just thankful it's the end of February and I can afford the time away from the farm."

Rebecca shook her head, not quite able to believe what she was hearing. It was his wedding day and he was worried about the farm. She knew she should be more understanding about Casey—after all, the child had just lost her parents—but she had expected, at the least, a wedding night.

"Anyway," Jake was continuing, totally oblivious to her shock. "You can move your stuff out to the farm, or wait until I get back and I'll help you move it." He stood slowly, wrapped his arms around her shoulders and gently pulled her up off her chair.

"Thanks for marrying me, Rebecca." His husky voice sent shivers running down her spine. Leaning down, he kissed her. It was hard and quick. His lips parted hers and his tongue thrust into her mouth, claiming it.

Before she even had a chance to respond, it was over and he was gone, her front door closing quietly behind him. His footsteps echoed on the steps and then there was silence. The sense of déjà vu was overwhelming. Sinking back down onto her chair, she stared at the door. Tears welled in her eyes and slipped slowly down her cheeks.

Rebecca felt sorry for herself for a whole hour. When she dragged herself into the bathroom and looked at her face in the mirror she almost started crying again. Her eyes were swollen and red, her nose sore. The throbbing in her head got worse. This was no way to spend her wedding day. She took two pain relievers, placed a cold wet cloth on her forehead, and lay down on her bed until lunchtime.

By the time she rose for lunch, she felt irritated. By three o'clock she was furious. *How dare he?* How dare he leave her on their wedding day without discussing it with her first? It was time for him to realize that he was no longer alone and that someone else was affected by his decisions. Namely, her.

As she filled the kettle with water and slammed it down on top of the stove, she made her decision. She would move out to the farm immediately. If she was going to relocate her business to the farm she would be wise to use the few days alone to set things up. When Jake arrived home with Casey, the little girl would be her top priority until they settled into some kind of a daily routine.

Yes, she decided as the kettle whistled and she made herself a cup of lemon tea, she would move out to the farm while Jake was away. She didn't have a whole lot of belongings to pack. The apartment had come furnished and she hadn't added much to it, preferring to sink all her spare money into her sewing business and her small savings account.

Pulling open a drawer, she dragged out a pen and pad of paper she kept handy for making her grocery list, and sat down at the table and sipped her tea. She needed to get organized. Other than her clothes, linens, and dishes—none of which there was much of—she had a small pine trunk that she'd bought for next to nothing at a yard sale. Her rocking chair, a large beautiful maple wood, had to go as well. Picking up the pen, she began to make notes to herself. Stopping now and again to think, she tapped the pen absently on the table and then resumed writing until she felt her list was complete.

It really was the perfect time to relocate, as February and March were her two slowest months. By April, when there was a demand for prom dresses and wedding gowns, she would be well established in her new location and into some kind of routine with Casey. There would be adjustments to make in both hers and Jake's schedule to accommodate the troubled little girl. Rebecca thrust her doubts aside, knowing she'd do whatever it took to be a good mother.

She was smart enough to know that she would have to cut back her hours to accommodate her ready-made family. She also knew that she would probably lose most of her smaller business by moving out of town.

Surprisingly enough, she was actually looking forward to her new life. It would be wonderful to be part of a family, to have something else to expend her energies on other than her work. Not that she didn't love her work, because she did, but she knew she needed more balance in her life. She had dreamed of having her own family for years and had almost given up believing it would ever really happen.

The afternoon flew by as she made her plans, and by the time she had finished supper, her anger towards Jake started to fade and her common sense attitude reasserted itself. She knew full well that Jake had married her to give his niece a home. It therefore didn't make any sense to leave Casey where she was any longer than necessary. The poor child was probably confused and afraid. The more she thought about it the gladder she was that Jake had left immediately for upstate New York. The frightened little girl needed her uncle now, and Rebecca knew that Jake took his responsibilities seriously.

She would use this time alone to settle into Jake's house. By the time he and Casey arrived, she would feel right at home. There would be plenty of time for her and Jake when they both had less on their minds. Time for the two of them to explore their new roles as husband and wife. She had dreamed about him for such a long time that a few more days of waiting wouldn't make much difference. After all, she was his wife now, and they had a lifetime to spend together.

Rebecca swung into action as soon as she finished washing her few supper dishes. A quick trip down the stairs to Greer's Grocery netted her the boxes she needed to start packing up her apartment. She was no stranger to hard work, or to going it alone, so by the time she went to bed at eleven o'clock that night all her materials and her machines were packed and sitting next to the cutting table, the only big item she owned. Her business was ready to be transported.

She lay awake in bed trying to estimate the number of boxes it would take to pack her personal belongings. Not as many as it had taken to pack up her small business. Her dishes were at a minimum, enough to cook and feed two. She owned few books, preferring to borrow from the library when she could. She owned a few compact discs and a small player, but not much else besides her clothes. Her linens and quilts would pack into her pine trunk. She saw no reason why she couldn't be ready to move by tomorrow afternoon.

It would be no problem to get a ride out to Jake's house with her stuff. Most of the people she knew owned trucks and Jake's farm was less than ten miles from town. Not that far at all. She was still making plans when she finally drifted off to sleep. Her last thoughts were to wonder where Jake was sleeping and if he would call her anytime soon.

Jake, sprawled out on the bed in his motel room, was wishing he had gotten there early enough to call Rebecca. The room was dark, except for a small ray of light shining in from a street lamp. It was just as well, he thought, as it was nothing to look at. Drab and dull, generic hotel. Cheap but clean—he just wished the bed had a few less lumps.

It was after midnight and he knew she would be in bed by now. He stuffed another pillow under his head and settled himself again. He hoped her day had been better then his. The long drive had been bad enough. Winter driving was never fun, but it was especially bad with so many idiots on the road. He'd never encountered so many reckless drivers in his life, all of who seemed intent on driving way too fast for the slippery road conditions. He'd passed more than one accident site on his way here. By the time he'd arrived at his hotel, he was tense and frustrated. But what he'd faced when he finally made it over to see his niece had been much worse.

Casey had not been doing well since he'd left her less than a week ago. She was quiet and withdrawn, hardly eating at all, according to Mrs. Bishop, her long-time babysitter. She had started having nightmares, but about what, Mrs. Bishop didn't know. Since her parents' death, Casey hadn't spoken a word. She would simply wake up crying every night. Now she was afraid to go to bed. It had broken his heart to see the frail little girl look up at him through eyes so much like his own. Except her green eyes had held such fear that his chest had tightened, making it hard for him to breathe.

Not knowing what else to do he had picked up the child and held her in his arms until she had fallen asleep. He hoped that once she was settled on the farm and more secure in her surroundings the nightmares would stop. It would only be a matter of time before she started speaking again. He just had to keep on believing that, he told himself as he turned onto his side. He stared out through the crack in the drapes, not really seeing anything in the darkness beyond.

Tomorrow, he would see the lawyers and start the process of settling his brother's estate. He found himself wishing he had brought Rebecca with him. Not that he needed her, he assured himself, but she would have been a great help with Casey. Rebecca, with her warm and caring ways, would be more at home with a child than he was. Hindsight was just that, however. Thinking about it wouldn't change anything.

He finally felt the tensions begin to leave his body, but just before sleep claimed him, he found his thoughts once again on Rebecca and himself. One thought occurred to him. *This was a heck of a way to spend his wedding night.*

Chapter Five

Rebecca unlocked the heavy back door and slowly pushed it open before taking her first step inside her new home. The big country kitchen greeted her. It was silly really, but she felt as if she were breaking and entering. She couldn't quite grasp the fact that this was her home now and she had every right to be there. Her musings were cut short by a male voice directly behind her.

"Where do you want these boxes?"

Rebecca turned and smiled. "I'm not sure. Set them down here while I look around. And thanks, Shamus, I appreciate the help."

The tall, lanky, young man returned her smile. "No problem at all, Rebecca. You know that. I'm glad I could help out."

Rebecca watched him return to the truck, which was pulled up as close to the back steps as it could get. Shamus O'Rourke was only a seventeen-year-old high school student, but he was already quite a man. Quick with a grin or a joke, but an incredibly hard worker, Shamus had worked with her at Greer's and she liked him very much.

She had also done some sewing for his sister, Dani Black, whom she had known in high school. They had drifted apart in the years that had followed, mostly due to the fact that they both had had to work hard and long to keep a roof over their heads. When Dani had come to her last spring about getting some drapes made, the two had renewed a friendship that was still flourishing. Rebecca, who had never had many friends, was still amazed that someone as well known and well liked as Dani wanted to be her friend.

Dani had been full of questions when she'd called to tell her about the wedding, and a little hurt that Rebecca hadn't told her about it before it happened.

"But, I would have been there," Dani had cried over the phone.

Rebecca hadn't wanted to admit she had been so unsure the wedding would actually take place, she had told no one about it beforehand. She'd promised Dani they'd get together soon and she would explain everything then. That gave her some time to figure out what she was going to tell the other woman.

Realizing that Shamus was back with another box, she shook off her thoughts and began to look around. She had been out to the farm quite a few times over the years, but she had never been past the kitchen itself. She came every spring to see the apple blossoms and again in the fall to pick apples. Jake had always let her pick as many as she had wanted as long as he got an apple pie out of each basket she took home. It had been a good arrangement and, as usual, Rebecca had grasped any excuse to spend some time with Jake.

After a quick tour of the downstairs, she returned to the porch. Shamus already had the large porch filled with boxes and was returning with another one as she sized up the growing pile.

"Okay. There's an empty room off the kitchen that's fairly large. I think it was probably the housekeeper's room, back when they had one years ago. All the boxes marked 'Store' can go in there. All the ones marked 'Kitchen' can be put on the kitchen counter, and all the ones marked 'Bedroom' can be left at the bottom of the stairs."

"Only you could be this organized, Rebecca. You were always a terror at the store." His eyes twinkled with good humor as he adjusted the box in his arms. "I'll take the store boxes since they're heavier and then I'll get the kitchen ones. You move the boxes with your clothes. They shouldn't be too heavy."

"Yes, sir." She smartly saluted before she picked up a box and headed for the bottom of the stairs. She was usually shy with strangers, but with the few friends she did have she was open and friendly.

In no time at all, it seemed, the boxes had been delivered to their appropriate destinations, and Rebecca was standing on the back porch once again.

"Thanks again, Shamus. I don't know what I would have done without you today."

Shamus waved her thanks away as he climbed into the front seat of the pickup. "No problem at all and if you need anything else just holler. Besides, now I have Dani's truck for the rest of the day and for tonight."

"Oh," she teased, "Hot date tonight?"

Shamus winked at her. "You bet. And by the way, Dani said to tell you she was only giving you a couple of days and she'd be out soon after that for a full accounting of the situation."

With that said he closed the door, started the engine, and pulled away, tooting the horn as he left. Rebecca stood there and watched the truck until it grew smaller and smaller and finally disappeared from sight. Turning away, she rubbed her hands over her arms, suddenly feeling very cold, as she went back into the house. No, not *the* house, she corrected herself. This was her home now, hers and Jake's.

Her quick look earlier had not satisfied her at all. Now that she was alone, she decided to explore. Creeping around, as if she expected someone to reprimand her at any minute for being here, she explored the downstairs first.

The kitchen was a dream come true. Large and airy, the walls were painted a creamy white and the floor was covered in hardwood planks. She smiled as she traced her finger over the pattern on the counter top. It was covered in an apple blossom print. Well, what else would you expect on an apple farm? The appliances were older, but she knew they would gleam when she polished their white surfaces.

She could already picture new drapes hanging from the window. Something in a green with apple blossoms on them to match the counter. Her herb plants would go nicely along the windowsill, and a few flowers wouldn't hurt either.

She peeked into Jake's office on her way to the living room, but she didn't venture inside his private domain. With its large oak desk and chair, brown leather sofa and matching chair, and papers stacked all around, it was a dark and wholly masculine room. She might be his wife, but she didn't feel comfortable entering this room when he wasn't there.

The living room was a little better, but it definitely lacked a feminine touch. Again the sofa and chair were covered in rich brown leather. The floor and the coffee table were hardwood, and the middle of the room was softened with an oval carpet in shades of green. Dark wooden bookshelves lined the wall on one side and were full of books haphazardly stacked. A television, VCR, and stereo filled another shelf facing the sofa.

A closer look at the books revealed an eclectic selection. There were books on everything from farming to woodcarving. There were popular titles of fiction and non-fiction, as well as some horror and mystery novels. The selection surprised her even though she knew it shouldn't. Jake was an educated man who spent a lot of time alone. It only made sense he would have varied interests.

It worried her a little. She had only finished high school while he'd had some college before he'd come home to run the farm. "Don't be silly," she spoke out loud as if to reassure herself. "Jake would never think less of you for your schooling." Still, it was a nagging thought.

His collection of CDs was eclectic, containing everything from country music to soft rock—and even some classical selections. It pleased her to see some of her favorites sitting on his shelf. At least they shared the same varied taste in music. Her few books and CDs would easily fit alongside his. In fact, she'd probably just set her own stereo up in her new work area. That way she would have music while she worked.

The dark brown drapes would definitely have to be replaced with something lighter, probably in a green print of some kind. That and a few throw pillows in the same material and in some contrast colors would do wonders for lightening the room. Her larger plants would look wonderful in here.

Satisfied with the changes she had in mind for the room, she headed upstairs. The stairs themselves were a lovely honey-toned wood with a blue runner, and she knew they would gleam when she polished them. A wall hanging she had done would look right at home on the cream-colored wall to the left of the staircase.

There were four bedrooms and a bathroom on the upper floor. She crept along the hall that was covered with the same blue carpet as the stairs, with the same warm-toned wood flooring peeking out on either side. Three of the bedrooms were simply furnished. Each had a rug in the center, and two of them held single pine beds while the other held a double. They all had a plain nightstand and a chest of drawers.

They wouldn't be too much trouble to fix up. A homemade quilt, some new drapes, and some pillow covers would brighten each room considerably.

Of course, Casey would have to help plan the colors for her own room. It would help her fit in more quickly and feel more at home. When it was filled with her own toys and clothes it would make her feel settled. Rebecca swallowed as her throat tightened. At least she hoped it would help Casey feel settled.

She reached the last door and hesitated. This was Jake's bedroom, which of course, meant it was now her bedroom as well. Slowly, she pushed the door open. "Oh my," she whispered in awe as she stepped inside.

It was simple, yes, but certainly not plain. The gigantic pine bed filled the room, and intricately carved apple blossoms adorned the headboard and footboard.

"It's like sleeping in an apple tree," she mused aloud, absolutely delighted with the bed.

The motif continued on the front of the two chests of drawers that stood along one wall, and on the front of the two nightstands that flanked either side of the bed. A blue rug covered the center of the room and blue drapes hung at the windows.

It was the largest of the bedrooms, but she had expected that. What she had not anticipated was that she would instantly fall in love with it. She had made herself a wedding ring quilt years ago and knew it was large enough to fit the king-sized bed. The interlocking rings on the quilt were all different shades of blue on a creamy background and would look spectacular spread across the mattress.

She ran her hands lovingly over the furniture as she crossed the room to the windows. It all looked a little dull right now, but she knew that with some lemon oil and elbow grease the bed, chest, and nightstands would soon gleam as they were meant to.

The view from the window was spectacular. Row upon row of dormant, naked apple trees hunched dark and gloomy, but oh how they would blossom in the spring. She could hardly wait until summer to fling open the window and have the smell of apple blossoms running through the house.

Rebecca sank into a straight back chair that sat next to the window. Absently, she noted it needed a seat cover to make it more comfortable and to add color to the room. She noticed her reflection in the window. Sitting there, with the room behind her, she looked right, she thought, as if she belonged there. She continued to stare out the window until the sun sank and the room turned dark.

She hadn't expected this at all. This sense of homecoming was like nothing she had ever experienced in her whole life. She knew in her heart she was where she was meant to be. She loved this house. No, it wasn't a house, but a home, a home for her and her family.

She felt the weight of the long day sink over her. She was tired. It had been difficult to leave her apartment, but what she had found here was something infinitely better. She pulled herself up from the chair, trudged downstairs, picked up one of her suitcases and dragged it and herself back upstairs. Everything else could wait until morning.

To her delight, there was a full bath off the master bedroom. A long hot bath helped to soak out some of the moving day kinks. Pulling on her flannel nightgown, Rebecca crawled into the large bed. It smelled like Jake, kind of woodsy and spicy, and she breathed his scent deep into her lungs. It made her feel closer to him, and for the first time since her wedding, she actually felt like a wife.

Smiling to herself, she hugged his pillow close to her in the darkness. Her body sank into the comfort of the mattress. Tomorrow, she would start acting like a wife. After all, she didn't have very long to get the house in shape before Jake and Casey came home.

She fell asleep thinking of all her plans, and just before sleep claimed her a little voice nagged in the back of her mind. *Why hasn't Jake called?*

Chapter Six

Jake breathed a deep sigh of relief as he pulled the truck up behind the old farmhouse. He felt a smile form on his face for the first time in days. He couldn't wait to see Rebecca, to wrap his arms around her and hold her. He laughed aloud. Who did he think he was kidding? He wanted to do more than hold her.

He hadn't called her since he'd left because he knew hearing her voice would have made him miss her more than he already did. And he had missed her. That had been a rather unpleasant surprise. One he hadn't expected. He had lain awake in his motel room night after night thinking about her, his body aching with need for her. It was probably a good thing the water in his motel bathroom had only run to cold showers.

He glanced at the little body slumped over on the seat next to him. Casey was so small and quiet sometimes he almost forgot she was in the truck with him. Almost. She was such a serious little girl, much too serious, as far as he was concerned. He wanted to see her smile and hear her laugh. His chest ached every time he looked at her, and he berated himself for neglecting to visit her before now—and that it had taken such a tragedy for him to get to know her.

Jake replayed the last few days in his mind as he put the truck in park and turned off the ignition. They had been filled with unpleasant surprises. His brother had been living on the financial edge for years, his lifestyle way above his means. An expensive car, clothing, jewelry, furniture, and weekend holidays had drained their cash and run up their credit cards. As a result, it had taken Jake and a lawyer a while to straighten out the mess of debts that had been left behind.

Jake silently thanked God that Optimum Electronics, the company his brother had worked for, had a mandatory life insurance policy program. It had taken all of the money from the policy, as well as from the quick sale of his sister-in-law's expensive jewelry, to satisfy all the creditors. There had been nothing left for Casey's future. Jake got angry all over again at the lack of care they had shown for their daughter. But she was his now and he would damned well provide Casey with whatever she needed.

He placed his hand on her small shoulder. "Time to wake up, honey. We're home."

Although he'd spoken softly, she jumped just as he feared she would. The look in her eyes was enough to make a grown man fall to his knees and weep. Such lost, large, green eyes.

"It's okay, Casey. We're home now."

The little girl looked at him and nodded. She picked up her doll, which had sat next to her for the entire trip, and waited for him to tell her what to do next.

It occurred to Jake that the doll hadn't been out of arm's reach ever since he'd given it to her. He had been appalled to learn that Casey had no toys. Her parents had never bought her any. According to her babysitter, her parents had said they had no money for toys she would only outgrow or break, so what was the point?

He'd never heard anything so ridiculous in his whole life. The next day he had gone out and bought her the soft rag doll, with its red woolen hair and green button eyes, she now clutched in her arms.

He was lifting her down from the truck when the back door slammed open.

"You're home! You're home!" Rebecca yelled as she raced down the back steps. She skidded to a halt when Casey scooted behind him and clutched his jacket for security.

"I thought you were supposed to bring me a little girl of my very own, Jake Tanner, and if you haven't got her, I'm sending you back to get her." Jake could see by the look in her eyes that she hoped she was doing the right thing.

"Come and meet your Aunt Rebecca," he coaxed as he gently pulled the little girl out in front of him.

Oblivious to the snow and cold, Rebecca knelt down in front of the child. "I'm glad to meet you, Casey," she said quietly. "I've been watching and waiting for you all week long. I baked some chocolate chip cookies for you if you'd like some after we get you settled into your new room."

Casey hugged her doll tighter and looked up at her uncle. When he nodded his okay, she stepped closer to Rebecca. It wasn't much, but it was a better start than he'd hoped for.

Rebecca stood slowly and brushed the snow off the knees of the jeans. She went up on her toes and planted a quick kiss on his cheek. Her cheeks were flushed and rosy when she stepped away from him. Gently clasping Casey's hand in hers, she led the child up the back steps and into the kitchen. "You can bring her things right upstairs when you're ready," she called over her shoulder as they disappeared inside.

Jake stood there, a little bemused by the greeting. Grinning, he rubbed his cheek where she'd kissed him. Rebecca was nervous of him. She must have been thinking about their wedding night as much as he had. That prospect sent his heart racing and his blood pounding through his veins as he hauled two suitcases out of the truck and followed them into the house.

His good feeling didn't last any further than the kitchen. The suitcases landed on the kitchen floor with a thump. Jake turned in a complete circle to take in the entire room. It was the same as a week ago, yet different. Green drapes with flowers covered the windows, and a bunch of small pots with herbs now occupied the shelf over the sink. To top it all, a tablecloth covered his table with an old Mason jar filled with flowers at the center. Jake felt his jaw tighten.

Some sixth sense made him check the room off the kitchen. Her entire shop had been set up in there. It was obvious she had been working when they had arrived. It certainly hadn't taken her long to make herself at home. He felt a headache starting in the back of his skull.

Jake took a deep breath to calm himself and made his way toward the stairs. He got as far as the living room and came to a dead stop. Good lord, what had she done to the place? There were colors and plants everywhere! It didn't even look like the same room. All his books and things were in different spots. Why did women always want to change the way a man had things? Obviously, his home hadn't been good enough for her the way it was. He forced his feet up the stairs, feeling his anger grow with every step he took.

By the time he got to the top of the stairs, his head was pounding, and it was almost impossible to keep his teeth from grinding together. He and Rebecca would talk later, but for now, he had to keep his temper in check until Casey was tucked in bed. She had been through enough without watching her new aunt and uncle fight. Jake prayed he'd make it through supper.

Supper was a quiet affair consisting of homemade beef stew and fresh baked bread. The fresh chocolate chip cookies and good coffee almost restored Jake's good humor. Almost.

He sat back in his chair feeling oddly content as he listened to Rebecca chat with Casey, or rather, at her. Rebecca didn't seem at all disturbed by the fact that the child didn't answer her back. It was a strange feeling for a man who had lived alone for so long to hear another voice at the supper table. Sitting here together, it felt almost as if they were a real family.

"I think I'll take Casey upstairs and tuck her into bed, Jake. She's falling asleep at the table." Rebecca reached for the young girl as she spoke. "We'll get you tucked into bed in no time and Uncle Jake will come up and kiss you good night." Rebecca winked at Jake over her shoulder as she left the room with Casey in tow.

Jake took his time washing up the dishes while he kept one ear open for the sounds of splashing of water and the murmur of Rebecca's voice that told him she was giving Casey a bath. He noticed his headache was almost gone as he finished the last dish. A quick swipe at the counter and he was finished. He headed upstairs just in time to catch the tail end of their conversation.

"As soon as you're settled in you can pick out the material you want for new drapes. We'll have all kinds of fun decorating your room, honey, just you wait and see." Rebecca sat on the side of the bed, gently smoothing Casey's hair back from her face.

"You all tucked in yet?" Jake propped himself up against the doorway of Casey's room.

Rebecca turned at the sound of his voice. "She's been waiting for you." Kissing the child goodnight, she stood up and stepped back to make room for him. Pushing away from the door, he crossed the room and bent down to kiss Casey's forehead.

"Good night, honey. Sleep tight and I'll see you in the morning." Casey closed her eyes and snuggled down under the covers. Jake heard Rebecca leave the room, her footsteps light as she headed back downstairs. He couldn't make himself leave right away. He just stood there and watched his niece for the longest time. She was sound asleep by the time he finally left the room.

Jake went back downstairs to the kitchen. He desperately needed another cup of coffee, and he and Rebecca needed to talk. He heard her rustling around in her new workroom and wondered if she was working. "Another coffee, Rebecca?" he called out as he poured himself one.

"Thanks," she replied as she came back into the kitchen and sat down at the table. "I'm glad Casey settled down easily. She's such a beautiful child, but she seems so lost."

Jake was glad for the opening and plunged headlong into what was on his mind. "Yeah, it's going to take a while for her to feel secure in her new home. You were real good with her tonight, but she's going to need a lot of your time."

Rebecca looked at him quizzically. "I know that. Why do you think I got my shop set up before you got back home with her? I knew she would need a lot of attention."

"So long as you spend as much time on her as you did on the house." The words popped out of his mouth before Jake could stop it.

"What's that supposed to mean?" It was obvious from the bewildered look on her face that Rebecca had no idea what he was talking about.

"I'm talking about all the stuff you did." Now that he'd started, he couldn't stop. "I didn't bring you here to redecorate. I married you to take care of Casey and I just want to make sure you've got your priorities straight." As Jake thought about all the changes that had taken place in his home, he found himself getting angry all over again. "It didn't take you very long to make yourself right at home."

Rebecca didn't move. In fact, it seemed as if she was hardly breathing. Her head was bowed and she said nothing. He filled the awkward silence. "What were you thinking?"

"I was thinking that I was your wife, Jake." Rebecca's voice shook with undisguised anger. "I thought you wanted to have a real marriage where I have a place here in our home, or should I say *your* home?" She raised her head and glared at him. "I thought you wanted a real family for all of us, a real home. I'm sorry if I overstepped myself. I didn't understand that you only wanted a live-in nanny for Casey. I won't make that mistake again." Rebecca finished her speech, quickly jumped up from the table, and ran upstairs. She was gone before he could even think to stop her.

Jake winced when he heard a door slam. He sipped his coffee, which suddenly tasted very bitter in his mouth. Picking up both cups, he walked to the sink and dumped what was left of his. Rebecca's coffee followed his down the drain. Making his way quietly around the downstairs, he locked the door for the night and turned off all the lights.

Reluctantly, he went up the stairs. The door to one of the spare rooms was closed and, he assumed, locked. Staring at the door, he swore softly. *How did things get this out of hand? This was supposed to be his wedding night.*

He raised his hand to knock, but then dropped it again. Turning, he went back down the hall to his own empty room.

The first thing he noticed was her nightgown lying across the end of the bed. Her scent seemed to fill the room. It seemed as if Rebecca had been planning to spend her nights with him, if all of her belongings in his room were any indication. If he'd kept his big mouth shut, he'd be in bed with her right now. His large hands would be sliding over her pale, slender body, cupping her small, firm breasts as he tasted them with his mouth. He'd be discovering what made her moan, what gave her pleasure, before sinking into her moist, welcoming heat. He groaned as he sat on the side of the bed and buried his face in his hands.

He went over their conversation again in his head. What had he said that was so bad? He supposed he shouldn't have lectured her about his expectations. It was just that he was so uncertain himself. What did he know about being married or raising a child?

Rebecca sure had been busy this week. Now that he thought about it, he had no idea how she had moved her things out here from town. He frowned at the thought of her carrying heavy boxes by herself. She had worked fast to set up her shop and had found time to fix up the place.

She was trying to belong here.

Oh Lord, how could he have been so stupid? He raked his hands through his hair in frustration. Fixing up the place and adding her touch to things was probably her way of showing him how committed she was to their marriage and to him.

Idiot that he was, all he'd seen was someone changing his house, not her trying to fit in. She had even made a few changes in here, he noticed. The furniture shined and new curtains hung at the windows. Jake grinned wryly. It seemed as if she'd spent the entire last week making drapes, as every room seemed to have a new set.

What had she been thinking about since their hasty marriage a week ago? Jake winced as he remembered the quick ceremony. There'd been no flowers, no friends, and none of the frills and extras most women demanded for a wedding. There hadn't been much time, but he honestly admitted to himself that he should have done more.

Maybe he could suggest a party to celebrate their marriage. Nothing too big, just a few close friends. Rebecca would like that. Or maybe he shouldn't assume she would. He would ask her what she wanted. Women liked to be asked. Damn, he felt like he was working blind here. Somehow, he'd try to make things right.

First things first, though. He knew he had a lot of fast-talking to do tomorrow to get Rebecca to forgive him. He had to convince her he wanted a real wife and not just a nanny for Casey. That's what had hurt her the most. He realized she had no idea he wanted her as much as he did. He'd done a poor job of showing her he cared for her.

He knew now that not calling her all week had definitely been a mistake on his part. Come to think of it, he'd never even told her why he hadn't called. She probably figured he hadn't thought about her. But the fact of the matter was that he'd spent way too much time thinking about her and picturing her in this bed next to him.

Jake pulled off his clothes, dropped them on the floor, and fell into bed wishing Rebecca were lying there next to him. As he took a deep breath, he caught her scent from the pillow. The scent of lavender and something womanly that was uniquely Rebecca drifted around him. It occurred to him that she must have been sleeping in his bed all week long when he was gone, and now that he was lying here she was gone. The irony made him grim.

He had a lot of explaining to do in the morning. He only hoped that Rebecca would understand and forgive him. The thought that she might not unsettled him. What if she packed up and left? The notion left him cold and he quickly pushed it out of his head. Rebecca was as committed to this marriage as he was or she would never have married him. She would forgive him. He would make her understand. He wouldn't let her leave him.

It was amazing how much his life had changed in such a short time. He was still planning what he was going to say in the morning when he fell asleep with the smell of Rebecca tickling his nostrils. His last conscious thought was of Rebecca. He hoped she was warm enough in the spare room, and he really hoped that she wasn't crying.

Chapter Seven

Images from the night before ran through her head like a never-ending nightmare. Upon waking, Rebecca had tried to open her eyes, but they seemed glued shut this morning. Raising one of her hands to scrub them, she winced in pain. "Oh, God," she moaned as she threw her flannel-covered arm over her eyes to shield them.

She had lain awake half the night, crying and thinking and thinking and crying, and still she had no answers. What should she do? She could run away and join the circus, she thought with a twinge of black humor. She already felt as if she was stuck on a high wire without a net. It seemed she couldn't go backward. Her only choice was to go forward. Scary.

In her heart, she knew she wouldn't leave. Casey needed her and she was already well on her way to loving the little girl. She had given her word to Jake and she had known when she married him that he didn't love her. She hadn't been misled.

It is too early in the morning to be lying to yourself, she thought as she threw back the covers and sat up on the side of the bed. The truth was she didn't want to leave because, when all was said and done, she still loved Jake and she was no quitter.

She needed to think. A shower, a nice long hot shower, was exactly what she needed. Dragging herself off the bed, she crept down the hall and into the bathroom.

A quick glance in the mirror almost gave her a heart attack. Her eyes were swollen and puffy and her cheeks were pale. She looked more like a lost child than Casey did.

"This won't do," she lectured the face in the mirror.

Flicking the taps in the shower, she quickly adjusted the temperature, stripped off her flannel shirt and stepped under the hot spray.

Her skin felt as if it was being stung with little needles, but it felt good all the same. She finally felt as if she might get warm again. Last night had left her feeling cold right to her very soul. Absently lathering the soap on her body, she considered her options.

Jake was a man, and she had forgotten that men, or at least the men she'd known, didn't like change around the house. Rebecca remembered how her father had hated for anything to change. She had tried her hand at rearranging the furniture in their small apartment once, and all she had gotten was yelled at and told to put everything back the way it had been.

Oh, why hadn't she remembered that before she'd started? But she knew why. Jake was nothing like her father, but she guessed that maybe most men felt that way about change. Her experience with men was extremely limited. How was she supposed to know these things?

Maybe she had insulted him by making him think that his home wasn't good enough for her to live in. She was horrified at the thought. And maybe, with all that had happened in the last couple of weeks, his home had been the one stable thing in his life. The one thing still under his control.

She started to shiver as the water turned cooler. She quickly washed her hair, rinsed off, and stepped out onto the bath mat. As she patted herself dry, she planned her strategy.

It would be easy to replace the new drapes with the old ones. She had all the curtains she'd replaced, folded and packed away in her workroom. She was grateful she hadn't gone ahead and cut them up into quilt squares.

The tablecloths and pillows could be easily removed and all the plants could be stuffed into her new work area. She knew it was still early, so there was a chance she might have the kitchen put back the way it was before Jake came down to breakfast.

She had to move slowly in her new relationship with Jake. It would break her heart, but she would have to move her things to the guestroom later. She would not infringe on his space.

She bit her lip to keep herself from crying. Crying solved nothing and gave you puffy eyes, and if hers got any worse she soon wouldn't be able to see. It was sad, but she didn't even know if he would care if she moved her things out of the master bedroom. She didn't even know if he wanted her at all.

"Enough," she muttered as she pulled on yesterday's clothes. She felt grungy dressing in clothes she had slept in, but that couldn't be helped. She wasn't going into Jake's room while he was still in it. She would change later when he was out doing chores around the farm.

She stopped and stared at herself in the mirror. She straightened her collar and smoothed her wet hair. Standing up to her full height, as short as that was, she tilted her chin up and marched out of the guestroom. She had a lot to do before breakfast, and somehow she would make Jake Tanner see that she had more to offer their marriage than a live-in nanny service.

The coffee was hot, the pancake batter was ready to pour onto the hot grill, and the biscuits were browning in the oven. Everything was ready. Or it would be, Rebecca thought, if she could just get these curtains changed before Jake came downstairs.

The plants had been stuffed into her studio. She would worry about removing the shelf later. The tablecloth had been whipped off the table and stowed away. The lovely needlepoint picture of an apple orchard, that she had completed over one long winter and had loving hung in her new kitchen, had been torn from the wall and ruthlessly stuffed away in her pine chest.

Now if she could only get these darn curtains down. They hadn't been this much trouble to put up. But the old adage was true—the more haste, the less speed.

"Gotcha." She felt triumphant as she pulled the end of the rod free from its hook and began to slide the curtain off.

If she'd had more time and sense she would have climbed down off the chair she was standing on instead of trying to work from on top of it. But she was in a hurry, so she balanced herself on the chair seat while she struggled with the four-foot rod.

It was times like this she hated being short. Short legs and short arms. It could be a real pain at times. "I can do this," she muttered under her breath. And she would have too, if it hadn't been for the noise behind her.

"What in the heck are you doing?" Jake stood in the doorway, arms crossed over his chest and legs spread wide as he glared up at her.

"Jake," she stammered. "I didn't hear you come down the stairs. I'm just taking down these curtains. Breakfast will be ready in a minute. The coffee is done, just help yourself." She knew she was babbling, but his timing couldn't have been worse.

Jake continued to stare at her, a perplexed look now entering his eyes, as he reached up to rub his jaw. "Why?"

"Why, what?"

"Why are you taking down the curtains?"

Rebecca replied in what she hoped was a breezy manner. "I decided I liked the old ones better."

Jake sighed with exasperation. "Rebecca, leave the damn curtains alone. We've got to talk."

"In a second. I'm almost finished," she replied as she continued to pull the material off the curtain rod. He started towards her, so she hurried even more, her hands yanking frantically at the fabric.

"Now, Rebecca."

She didn't know how it happened. One minute she was wrestling with the curtains, the rod and the chair, the next, she felt herself suddenly airborne as Jake jerked her off her feet and into his arms.

The curtains and rod landed on the floor in a heap as Rebecca threw her arms around his shoulders—just for balance, she assured herself. Her heart pounded and she couldn't swallow because of the lump in her throat. It felt good and right to be held by Jake.

His arms tightened around her until they were almost painful. She felt his heart pounding beneath his shirt. "Don't you have better sense than to try and change drapes while standing on a chair? It's a miracle you didn't fall off and break a leg or something." He glared down at her as he spoke.

Rebecca struggled to get out of his grasp. "How do you think the drapes got up there to begin with?"

Jake dropped into a kitchen chair, his arms tightening even more around her. "You could have been hurt," he muttered and buried his face in her hair.

Rebecca stopped struggling. Jake had been afraid for her. The realization was a startling one. She had been alone for such a long time, she didn't expect anyone to worry about her. It made her feel warm inside to realize that Jake did, in his own way, care for her.

"I'm all right, Jake." She pulled away enough so she could look at him, but she made no attempt to leave his lap.

Jake sighed and looked around the kitchen. She had been busy this morning. The wall by the table was plain again, the table itself was bare and the window where the plants and new drapes had been was also empty. In fact, Jake laughed inwardly without humor, it resembled his old life: barren.

"Rebecca I need to talk and I need for you to listen to me. Will you please hear me out?"

"All right." She tried to move off his lap to sit at another chair, but he tightened his grip around her. She settled quietly back into his embrace.

"Yesterday, I said and did some things I shouldn't have." He gave her a wry smile. "Yesterday? No, it seems like I've been making mistakes all week long." He paused to collect his thoughts, wanting them to come out right.

"I haven't been very fair to you this past week. First, I spring this whole marriage thing on you, and your wedding day is nothing more than a quick ceremony and breakfast. Then I leave you all alone to move out here. And if that wasn't enough, then I get mad at you for fixing up the house." He took a deep breath at the end of his long speech.

"It's okay, Jake," Rebecca started to interrupt, but he shushed her by placing a finger over her mouth.

"Let me finish, honey." When she nodded, he removed his finger and continued. "The truth is, I guess I didn't think about all the adjustments you were making to your life. I was only thinking about the changes in my life, and that's unforgivable."

She felt small and frail in his arms, but he knew she had a backbone of steel. The sight of her removing the curtains she had made for his home, with her own two hands, had made his heart ache. That she felt she had to take them down was telling, and he began to wonder if he would be able to repair the damage his thoughtless words had inflicted.

When she started to reply he shushed her again. "I meant what I told you when we got married. I want this to be a real marriage. I respect you more than any other woman I've ever known and I know you won't neglect Casey. I guess I was just angry at the whole world last night and I took it out on you." He gently cupped her chin and tilted her head back until she was looking straight into his eyes. "Will you forgive me?"

He waited for what seemed an eternity and finally she nodded her head. Leaning forward, he gently kissed her swollen eyes. "I'm sorry I made you cry, honey. I don't mind all the fancy new stuff in the place."

If it made her feel more at home, he'd darn well make himself get used to it. "Will you put it all back?"

He watched her carefully, hoping he had said the right things. Hoping she would give them another chance.

"Can I talk now?" A small smile shaped Rebecca's lips. At his nod she continued. "I'm as guilty as you are. I never stopped to think that you might have had enough chaos in your life in the past couple of weeks. It never occurred to me that I might insult you by changing your home. I never meant to imply your home wasn't good enough the way it was."

She ran her hand lightly across his tousled hair. "We've both got a lot of new things to get used to if this marriage is going to work."

Rebecca took a deep breath as she prepared to begin again. She knew Jake cared for her; that much was obvious from his apology this morning. Jake wasn't a man who made flowery speeches or said things he didn't mean. He was in earnest, and since he was, she had only one choice she could make. "I'd like to begin again if you do. We can pretend that we just got married this morning and go on from here. What do you say?"

A smile spread slowly across Jake's face. "I say, good morning, Mrs. Tanner."

Rebecca felt like she might burst, she was so happy. As she leaned toward him, she saw his lips lowering to hers. Perfect, she thought.

The sound of a bell made them both jump, and the sound of little feet running down the stairs made Rebecca leap off Jake's lap.

"My biscuits!" she cried, pulling the oven door open as she dragged on the oven mitts. She hauled the pan out of the oven and inspected the contents. "They're edible. We'll be able to eat them for breakfast after all."

Casey stood in the kitchen doorway, uncertainty written all over her face, until Jake reached out for her. "Come here, honey." That was all it took for the little girl to run to her uncle.

"Look what Aunt Rebecca made for breakfast. Do you like biscuits?" Casey nodded shyly and Jake laughed. "Well, lets get that fancy cloth back on the table so we can eat those fine looking biscuits."

"We've got pancakes and syrup, too. I hope you're both hungry."

Jake met her eyes over the top of Casey's head and she smiled back in understanding. They had weathered their first fight. It was a good start to their first day as a family.

They spent the day like many other families do, but it felt different and special because it was their first one as a family. Rebecca dressed Casey warmly in two pairs of leggings, a fancy pink sweater, and a faux fur-trimmed long coat.

The girl's clothing had appalled her. Casey had a small suitcase of clothing, all of good quality, but there were no play clothes. All of it looked like it was for church on Sunday. When she had questioned Jake he had told her he would tell her about it later, so she had dressed Casey in what she had.

They had walked through the barren apple orchards, her on one side of Casey and Jake on the other, each of them holding on to one of the little girl's hands. Casey had been so excited. At first she had walked slowly and stayed close, but as the morning progressed she had run on the snow-covered paths, her cheeks red from the cold and exercise.

Hot chocolate in front of a roaring fire had followed as the three of them had curled up on the sofa in the living room to watch a kid's movie on television. All in all, simple things, but as Rebecca stared at the man and child curled next to her, she was filled with a contentment that she had never known in her life.

Chapter Eight

"She's finally asleep."

Jake looked up from the *Jamesville Chronicle*, the weekly newspaper, as Rebecca's tired voice broke the silence in the kitchen. "You'd think Casey would have been tired after the day she had." He folded the paper and pushed it aside.

"She was overtired, I think." Rebecca poured both herself and Jake a fresh cup of coffee and joined him at the table, settling comfortably into her chair. "You were going to tell me about Casey's lack of clothes."

Jake scrubbed his hands over his face and sighed. "Yeah." He took a quick sip of coffee as if to fortify himself for the coming conversation. "Hank and Celine lived fast and hard, and well above their means. They seemed overly concerned with appearances, and with what their so-called friends thought."

Jake paused and Rebecca stayed silent, aware of his mixed emotions.

"Honestly, Rebecca, I think they had Casey because every other corporate family has at least one kid. They seemed to treat her like a doll that they dressed up to show off to company but otherwise left with her nanny. She doesn't have any play clothes or any toys. It's scary sometimes how she just sits there like she's waiting for someone to tell her what to do."

Rebecca reached out and covered Jake's work-worn hand with her own. "She seems healthy even if she's not talking, and as for the rest, well, we'll take care of it. We'll make sure she has the best childhood she can have from here on in."

"I know we can't change anything, but I can't believe Hank turned out that way. We didn't always get along but he was raised better than that." Jake took another sip of coffee and continued. "There's nothing left for Casey now that all their debts are paid off. The only decent thing they did for her was to name me as her legal guardian in their will. I can't bear to think of her left with strangers because they couldn't find any relatives."

"She's here with us now and that's all that matters," Rebecca declared. She gave his hand a reassuring squeeze before leaning back in her chair. "We'll go shopping tomorrow and get her some play clothes and some books and toys, and then she and I will work on her bedroom. The quicker she feels like it's hers the quicker she'll settle in."

"You're good for her and good to her, Rebecca. Thank you for that," Jake replied solemnly. "I meant what I said this morning. I know you won't neglect Casey. I know you'll always put her well-being first."

Rebecca's face glowed as she absorbed his praise. "Thank you for your trust. Besides, how could anyone not love her? She's such a lovely child." Her hands toyed with her mug as she asked the question that had been on her mind all day. "Jake, should we take her to see a doctor? I mean, it's been a while since her parents' deaths and she's still not talking."

Jake propped his elbows on the table and rested his chin on his hands. "I took her to her own doctor before we left New York and he said that physically there's nothing wrong with her. All we can do is wait. He figures when she's feeling secure and ready, she'll talk, and not before."

Rebecca sighed dejectedly, "I feel helpless not to be able to do something to help her."

"We're doing all we can, honey," Jake replied. "And now I want to change the subject." He looked at her with a gleam in his eye.

"What?" she asked cautiously.

"It's getting kind of late and tonight's our wedding night. Don't you think it's time to go to bed, Mrs. Tanner?" He rose from the table and held out his hand.

Suddenly, Rebecca found it hard to breathe. All day long she had been pushing this moment to the back of her mind, not wanting to deal with the reality of their marriage. Now, he was forcing it out in the open, no longer allowing her to avoid the inevitable.

So much had happened since their wedding day. So much time had passed that she was incredibly nervous. Her legs were trembling as she pushed back her chair and stood. She ignored his proffered hand, knowing hers were shaking. She needed some time to compose herself.

"I'll go on up and get ready for bed. You lock up," she answered in what she hoped was a calm, matter-of-fact voice. Without giving Jake time to answer, Rebecca turned and fled up the stairs and into Jake's room, now her room as well.

She grabbed a nightgown and hurried into the master bathroom. She wanted to be changed and in bed before he got here. It would be easier on her already-shot nerves that way.

It was fine to want something, but much harder to get it. Her hands wouldn't cooperate. You'd think she'd never unbuttoned a blouse before, her fingers fumbled so badly with the fastenings. She tore off her socks and jeans and then unsnapped her bra. She got lost in the folds of her nightgown before she found the holes for her arms and her head. Finally, she was ready.

She jerked the bathroom door open, ready to dive into bed, and ran smack into a hard male body.

"There's no need to hurry, honey, we've got all night," Jake chuckled as he caught her in his strong arms.

Rebecca wished she could just sink into the floor and disappear. So much for being calm and matter-of-fact about their sleeping together. She was absolutely mortified. She felt the heat in her cheeks and knew her face was beet red.

He hugged her tight as if sensing her discomfort. "You climb on into bed and I'll be out in a minute." He offered her a comforting squeeze before releasing her and giving her a small push toward the bed.

When the door to the bathroom closed behind him, she didn't need a second push. She dived for the bed, jerked the covers back, jumped in, and pulled the blankets over her head.

This was not the way she had pictured starting her wedding night. She didn't know quite how she thought it would happen, but she had never imagined having to deal with all these irritating little things, like getting undressed and deciding who got the bathroom first. She had magically pictured the two of them in bed together. It had all been perfectly natural in her dreams. She hadn't had to deal with pesky buttons and feelings of inadequacy.

"I know you're in there somewhere." Jake's voice put an end to her meandering. He'd certainly finished quickly in the bathroom. She felt his stare through the little mound of bed covers. She knew he could tell she was nervous, but did he have any idea just how nervous? She rubbed her sweaty palms across the sheet.

The bed shifted as Jake climbed under the covers, and she clutched the sheet tighter. She hated feeling stupid like this. She didn't know what to do next. Should she make the first move, or should she wait for Jake? Fortunately, for her state of mind, he took the decision out of her hands. He reached out and found her in the darkness.

"Come here, Rebecca," Slowly, he tugged the sheet from her nerveless fingers and pulled her into his embrace. He tucked her head against his shoulder and wrapped his arms around her. She was stiff at first, but gradually as he ran his hands up and down her back in a soothing motion, she began to relax.

"There's nothing to worry about, honey. I won't do anything you don't want me to, and we've got all night." Jake assured her. She hoped he was right about that last pronouncement.

"I just feel silly about everything," Rebecca wailed, hardly recognizing her own voice. "I mean, I'm not afraid of you and I trust you, but I'm nervous."

"Perfectly understandable, honey. It's our first time together." Jake tilted her head up until she was looking at him. "It'll be good, Rebecca, so good." He lowered his head and covered her lips with his. He lightly tasted her lips before probing for entrance, and when she parted her lips for him, he took possession of her mouth.

Rebecca had been kissed before, but not like this. This was all consuming. All she tasted was Jake. He tasted slightly of mint toothpaste and coffee. She loved the taste. His lips devoured hers as if he couldn't get enough of their sweetness.

Kissing Jake was unlike anything else she had ever done in her life. Her hands forged their own path up his back, testing the tautness of his skin and the play of his muscles as his arms moved up and down her back in a similar motion. His hand moved to her breast, gently squeezing and shaping it. She moaned and arched her back, pushing her breast deeper into his hand. She needed more. Wanted more.

"Honey, let's get this nightgown off." Jake was already pulling it over her head as he spoke.

Rebecca was shocked to find herself naked except for her underwear, and then they were gone, whisked from her body in one quick motion. Even more shocking was the realization that he was naked as well. She had been so nervous that she hadn't realized he had removed all of his clothing before climbing into bed. But when he pulled her back in his arms, she ceased to think at all.

Jake's hands roamed all over her as if he was fascinated by all the curves and hollows of her body. His hands moved over her breasts, shaping them with his fingers, and playing with the tips. She moaned softly.

His lips followed his hands and he took one of her nipples into his mouth, gently tasting. She slipped her hand behind his head, holding him closer as he switched to her other breast to give it equal attention.

Rebecca felt like she was in the middle of a whirlwind. So much was happening and there was no time to think. All she could do was feel and hang on tight to Jake. She trusted him to keep her safe, but the feelings filling her were foreign, yet delicious. The things he was doing with his mouth made her ache with pleasure, and she arched her hips, rubbing her mound against his erection.

She moved against him again, gasping as his hand swept down between her legs, probing and testing her readiness. She was more than ready for him. The way he touched her was pure magic.

"Part your legs, honey," he whispered in her ear as he trailed kisses down the side of her neck. When she complied, he settled himself between her legs and took her face in his hands. Slowly, he started to push into her. She made a seductive little motion with her hips, unable to stop herself, and he drove quickly into her in one stroke. Filling her.

She froze and tried to pull away. The pain of his entry had driven away the haze of passion that had absorbed her. She knew the first time was supposed to hurt, but she had forgotten that small detail in the face of all the pleasure.

His voice was filled with disbelief. "Why didn't you tell me you were a virgin?"

Rebecca was hurt to the core and tried to push him away. "Why would you think I wouldn't be?" she cried. His arms tightened around her and he gently controlled her struggles.

Jake rested his forehead on hers as sweat dripped from his face. "You're so beautiful, I figured some guy would have..." he trailed off. "Enough talk."

He captured her mouth in a searing kiss as he carefully began to thrust. Her body began to match his rhythm as if she had no control over it. He immediately reached between their bodies to stroke her, gently at first and then more firmly. Their bodies began to move faster and harder. She stopped trying to control her own body and instead concentrated on pulling him closer to her.

Rebecca knew her body was reaching for completion, but she wasn't sure how to help herself. All she knew was that she'd die if he stopped.

"Jake." Her voice was filled with tension and a little fear. Fear that she wouldn't get what she desperately needed.

"Let yourself go, honey I've got you," Jake commanded as he surged heavily into her. Her body began to convulse. Wrapping her legs around his waist, she clasped him tight to her as he came deep within her. He yelled as he thrust one final time before collapsing on top of her. At the last second, he managed to shift most of his weight off her upper body, and they both lay there gasping for breath.

When Rebecca came back to herself she wasn't sure what to feel. She couldn't believe she was the same woman who had clung and moaned and demanded. No one had ever told her making love would be like this. This sense of closeness with another person, the feeling of belonging, the sheer rightness of their being together astounded her.

She felt Jake start to move away from her and tried to keep him there, but he shifted off her. "I'm too heavy for you, honey."

Rebecca floated in a haze of contentment for a while before she became aware of the almost unnatural quiet. The longer Jake lay there in a brooding silence the more nervous she became. The happiness that had wrapped her in its grasp was quickly dissipating.

She shifted uneasily in the bed, no longer comfortable. What if he hadn't enjoyed it as much as she had? What if she was no good at this? She couldn't stand the silence any longer. "Jake, are you okay?"

"Yeah." He turned onto his side to face her.

"Was it okay?"

He sighed, but wrapped an arm around her and pulled her close. "I should be asking you that question. Are you okay? Did I hurt you, honey?"

"I'm fine and you didn't hurt me too much, not that I noticed much after we started." She felt a little sore, but she decided it was worth it.

Leaning down, he kissed her forehead. "I'm glad you enjoyed yourself."

Sensing his lightened emotions, she felt the corners of her own mouth turn upward as her good mood returned. "I enjoyed it lots."

Totally relaxed and comfortable in his arms, she lay there replaying it all over and over in her head until she drifted off to sleep. Sex with Jake had been more than she had ever imagined it would be, but as naïve as she was, she sensed it had not been all it could be. He had distanced himself from her at the end when they should have been closest.

She knew the biggest factor for her was that she loved him with all her heart. But for a while, there had been such incredible closeness between them, pure togetherness, as their bodies had moved as one. It was something to build on. She could wait. For now it was enough.

Jake finally relaxed as he felt Rebecca drift off to sleep. Making love with Rebecca had shaken him to his very core.

Never in his entire life had sex been this emotional and explosive. Never had he felt this physically in sync with another person. It was as if she filled some empty part of him, and frankly, that scared the shit out of him.

No way would he allow this to happen. He'd enjoy her body, he'd respect her, and he'd like her. But there was no way would he ever allow himself to love her.

In his experience, women didn't stay. His mother had always hated the farm and she'd certainly made sure his father knew that she was miserable every single day of their married lives. His father had tried hard to please her, but it had never seemed to be enough. As her son, he had tried his best to make her happy, but he didn't remember her ever being happy, not one single day.

He'd thought he'd been in love once, back in college, but she'd shown just how much she loved him when he'd told her that his father had died and he had to go back to the farm. She couldn't dump him fast enough. *No!* There was no way he'd make himself vulnerable again.

Their marriage was the partnership of two people committed to a common goal. They would raise Casey and have a good marriage, a long marriage. There was no place here for that fickle emotion known as love.

Pleased with his common sense analysis, Jake snuggled Rebecca closer to him. It felt good to have her in his arms, in his bed. Sleep quickly claimed him.

Chapter Nine

The bell tinkled merrily as Jake ushered his new family into Jessie's Diner, bringing a shot of cold February wind with them. Jessie looked up and smiled automatically as they entered. Her smile grew even brighter as she recognized them and she hurried out from behind the counter to greet them.

"Come in. Come in. How is married life treating you? Good, I'd say, by the look of you." Jessie answered her own question, not giving them time to speak. She stopped as she saw the beautiful little girl peeking out from behind Jake. "And who is that hiding behind you?"

"This is my niece, Casey. She's come to live with us now. Isn't that right, Casey?" Jake reached down to lift the little girl into his arms as he spoke. Casey gave a timid nod and hid her face in the soft collar of Jake's winter jacket.

Jessie's eyes softened with pity as she looked at the child. Everyone in Jamesville had heard about Jake's brother and sister-in-law dying in that horrible accident. "You must all be cold. Find a seat and I'll bring you some coffee. Would you like some hot chocolate, Casey?" Jessie waited for Casey to reply, but her face remained hidden.

"I'm sure she would love some hot chocolate, Jessie." Rebecca undid her scarf and stamped the snow from her boots.

Jake led them to a window booth and stood Casey on the seat while he helped her out of her coat. As soon as he removed her coat, she scooted in by the window, sat down on the seat, and folded her hands in her lap.

He glanced over at her, and Rebecca saw the helpless look in his eyes. It had been like this all morning. The child was so well behaved it was downright scary. It was as if she was afraid of doing anything wrong, so she did nothing at all.

"Give it time, Jake," Rebecca murmured, instinctively responding to his gaze of despair. She knew what he was thinking because the same doubts plagued her mind. Before she could say anything to ease his mind, Jessie came bustling up to the table with the hot drinks and the menus.

"The soup today is chicken, and there's apple and cherry pie as well." It didn't need to be said that it was all fresh or homemade, since Jessie wouldn't have it any other way and her customers knew it.

"I think I'll have a piece of cherry pie. What about you, Jake?" Rebecca pushed her menu aside without looking at it. Jessie's cherry pie was too good to pass up.

Jake looked at Casey first. "Do you like cherry pie?"

Casey appeared to think for a moment. Her little face was a study in concentration. Finally, she shrugged her shoulders, as if uncertain.

"Do you like apple pie?" Jake's tone was soft as he ran his hand lightly over her silky hair.

Seeming more certain this time, Casey nodded and smiled.

"Casey will have apple pie and I'll have a slice of cherry." Jake gave Jessie the order as he handed the menus back to her. Seemingly without thought, his arm wrapped around Casey's shoulders.

Rebecca sipped her coffee and sighed as she watched the two of them together. This was exactly what the little girl needed—some quiet, family togetherness.

They been busy today from the moment they awoke. Well, almost from the moment they'd awoken. She felt her cheeks heating up as she remembered waking up, wrapped in Jake's arms, this morning. One good morning kiss had led to another and, before she'd managed to catch her breath, Jake had made love to her in a slow, unhurried way that had brought tears to her eyes. It made her warm just thinking about it.

Jake had spent the morning doing chores around the place. Or at least she assumed that was what he was doing. She wasn't quite sure what he did, only that he was gone for a couple of hours. She had a lot to learn about being a farmer's wife, she supposed.

Casey and she had spent the time choosing the material for Casey's new bedroom curtains. It had taken her quite a while to convince the child she could pick out whatever color she liked out of the stacks of material in Rebecca's workroom, and in the end she had chosen a bright lemon yellow.

Later, the two of them had made lunch, which had been an education for both of them. Rebecca has pulled a kitchen chair over to the counter for Casey and allowed her to spread butter on the bread for the ham and cheese sandwiches they had made to go with the chicken noodle soup. Casey was very precise in her movements, and Rebecca had helped her only when necessary. She felt children needed a chance to learn things on their own, but she made sure she was there in case the little girl required any help.

Casey seemed to enjoy herself, smiling frequently, and looking to Rebecca for approval. After lunch, Rebecca let her help clean up by bringing her own dishes to the counter. Casey had surprised her when she'd taken a cloth and tried to wipe the table down, stretching as far as her little arms would reach. When they were all cleaned up from lunch, the three of them had climbed aboard the truck and headed to town to do some essential shopping.

Rebecca was brought back to the present when Jessie placed her cherry pie in front of her. Casey and Jake already had theirs in front of them. "Thank you. It looks delicious." The older woman smiled and went to pour coffee for another customer.

"I think our shopping trip was a success, don't you, Casey?" Rebecca hoped including her in all the conversations might make her comfortable enough to speak.

Casey looked up from her plate and smiled shyly.

"I'd say it was a success if all those bags you stashed in the truck are any indication." Jake's eyes twinkled as he winked at the child. He cut her pie into little pieces for her and for a few minutes there was no conversation as they all filled their empty stomachs. The only noise was the scrape of their forks on the plates as they tucked away the delicious pie.

Jake was filled with a wave of contentment as he watched Rebecca and Casey. It was a strange feeling for him. He was used to being alone, and he was happy enough in his own company, but this was different. It was an emotion deep inside of him that insisted this was the way things should be.

That thought set off warning bells in his brain. He didn't need any of it, he assured himself. He didn't need anybody, but it was his responsibility as a man to take care of his family. Yes, that had to be the reason for this sense of contentment. Nothing more. He noticed Rebecca staring at him and grinned when she started blushing after he returned her look.

The door to the diner opened and the rush of cold air carried another couple into the warmth. The man was tall, dark, and dangerous-looking with a scar running down the left side of his face. His arm was wrapped securely around the woman at his side as he ushered her inside. The woman was beautiful in the way that only pregnant women can be. Her long hair was tied back in a loose braid and a smile filled her face as she spotted them.

"Rebecca! Jake! It's great to see you. I've been meaning to get out to visit." Dani Black hurried over to the table, as best as she could, considering she was six and a half months pregnant.

Jake stood as they reached the table, nodded at Dani and stuck his hand out to the man at her side. "Burke."

"I hear congratulations are in order." Burke Black smiled at Jake as they shook hands.

"Thanks. Would you like to join us?" Jake motioned to the booth.

Dani smiled. "We'd love to, but Patrick is joining us any minute and I don't see enough of that brother of mine these days since he's been away at school." She turned to Rebecca. "I called you a couple times last week, but you were always out. It's not fair that I had to get all my news from Shamus. I promise I'll try to get out to see you some time this week."

Rebecca smiled at her friend's enthusiasm. "You come out whenever you want. Casey and I will be home." She turned to Casey to introduce her, but the little girl was practically buried behind Jake's back. She turned back to Dani. "The little girl trying to hide behind Jake is Casey. She's a little shy right now."

"Hello, Casey." Dani spoke as if nothing was out of the ordinary. "I'll see you when I visit this week." She was rewarded with a flash of green eyes as Casey peeked out from behind Jake and then quickly turned away again.

"Congratulations again, Jake. Rebecca." Burke ushered his wife to an empty booth in the corner. Dani gave a little wave as she allowed her husband to seat her.

"It's okay, honey. You can come out now." Jake spoke in a low, even voice as he looked down at his niece.

Slowly, she moved away from him, quickly peeking up at him from beneath her lashes. Jake smiled at her reassuringly. "It's okay, honey," he repeated. He watched her as she relaxed and concentrated on eating her pie, one small piece at a time.

"I didn't know you and Dani were good friends." Meeting the other couple had made him realize he didn't know everything about Rebecca's life. He was ashamed and a little uncomfortable to admit that up until now he hadn't been real interested. She'd always been there when he needed her or wanted to spend time with her, but he'd never thought much about what went on in her life when he wasn't there. It made him feel more than a little self-centered. She was his wife now; he should at least know who her friends were.

"Dani and I went to school together until she dropped out in the last year to go to work to support her brothers. We lost track after that. You know how it is. Life gets in the way. Anyhow, after she married Burke last year, she called me about making some drapes for their new house and we kind of renewed our friendship. We get together once or twice a month for coffee and talk at least once a week on the phone. It's nice to have a female friend." Rebecca popped the last piece of cherry pie into her mouth, and Jake wondered what cherries would taste like on her lips.

"I don't know them well, but I met them both when I sold Dani my old truck about a year ago." Jake stopped fantasizing about cherries for a moment. Something Dani had said had stuck in his mind. He wasn't jealous, he told himself, merely interested. "Who's Shamus?"

Rebecca laughed. "You remember Shamus O'Rourke. He's Dani's younger brother. I used to work with him at Greer's. He helped me move my stuff out to the house in Dani's truck." She picked up her coffee and took another sip. "Come to think of it, it was the truck you sold her that moved my stuff out to the house. Funny how these things work out," she mused.

The little sound of distress from the corner stopped them both cold. They both turned toward Casey and were stunned when the little girl shrank back from them, pulling herself into the corner of the booth. Her little hands were clasped tight to her chest.

Jake spoke in a soothing voice. "What's wrong, honey?" When she didn't answer he tried again. "Did you say something?" *God, please let her speak*, he thought as he waited. He was appalled when she said nothing and two fat tears rolled down her cheeks.

Casey scrubbed frantically at the front her sweater.

Jake held his breath, waiting to see if she would speak. It was extremely frustrating trying to understand what went on in her child's mind or to guess what she was feeling. He gently reached out and stilled her hands. "What's wrong, honey?" he asked again, his voice harsh with his frustration at his inability to understand.

Casey took a shaky breath, lifted her head, and pointed at her sweater as if to show him something.

Jake and Rebecca looked at each other. A pie stain. She was upset over a piece of spilled pie. It was all Jake could do not to cry. He saw the tears in Rebecca's eyes as she grabbed a napkin and gently took hold of the sweater and rubbed the stain. "It's not too bad at all. We'll wash it right out when we get home and it will be as good as new."

Casey looked at him as if she was surprised they weren't mad at her. Was she afraid that if she was any trouble, she would be sent away? Jake didn't know what Casey was thinking, but he knew he had to reassure her. He lifted her carefully into his arms and hugged her to him, wanting her to feel safe. His patience was rewarded when she threw her small arms around him and held on to him with all her might.

"Come on, let's go." His voice was husky as he threw some money on the table to pay the bill. He let Casey out of his arms long enough to zip her back into her coat, and with her cradled in one arm, and the other around Rebecca, they left.

They were quiet on the drive back to the farm, each pondering the afternoon's events. Even though nothing much had really happened, they all felt as if they had taken a huge step. They had passed their first crisis together as a family.

Casey was snuggled between them and when he glanced down at her, she was sound asleep. The dried tear stains on her cheeks were a testament to the child's trauma and emotions. He felt as drained as she did.

Jake tried not to think too much about things. He wanted to take one day at a time, but he felt as if something deep inside him had shifted. This afternoon, he'd wanted to fix whatever was wrong and make Casey and Rebecca smile again. He didn't want anything to ever hurt them. For the first time in his life he'd felt like a husband and a father. Surprisingly, it was a good feeling.

Chapter Ten

As the days passed, they fell into a routine, of sorts, around the old farmhouse. Dani came out to visit several times, but Rebecca kept the conversation general and lighthearted, not willing to delve too deeply into her marriage with the other woman. Jake spent his days doing chores around the farm, things like checking the trees for any weather damage, making repairs to the farm equipment, and toiling in the workshop he had built in the loft of the barn. Rebecca wasn't quite sure what he did when he was out there, but since he never offered any information, she never asked. While Jake continued to be an attentive husband in the bedroom at night, he seemed to distance himself from her in the daytime.

"He just needs some time," she muttered under her breath. It was the mantra she uttered at least a dozen times a day. Jake might be distant and reserved with her, but he spent a lot of time every evening with Casey.

Casey, on the other hand, was a joy to spend time with, and she was Rebecca's shadow during the daytime. The two of them had selected a wallpaper border of wildflowers from Hammers and Nails, the local hardware shop, and had an enjoyable afternoon pasting it on the cream-colored walls. The paper border was about halfway up the wall, at waist height, enabling Casey to see and touch it whenever she wanted to. Casey spent so many hours admiring the colorful flowers that Rebecca had already decided they were planting a flower garden in front of the house as soon as the spring frost had disappeared.

Another day, the child had sat wide-eyed in the sewing room, watching as Rebecca had sewn bright yellow drapes and a dazzling yellow comforter cover for the little girl's bed. Material with wild flowers trimmed the curtains and the new pillowcases. It filled Rebecca with such joy to watch her solemn little face light up with pleasure. Although she still did not speak, Rebecca knew Casey was happy.

She felt the tug on her shirt and looked down at the child waiting impatiently at her side. "Shall we tackle the living room next, Casey?"

Casey returned her smile, picked up her dust cloth, and waited while Rebecca gathered up the cleaning supplies and some more dust rags.

Rebecca continued talking to Casey as if the child was responding. And in a way she was. Rebecca knew she was getting better at deciphering Casey's emotions through her gestures and facial expressions. She felt it was best to just act as if everything was normal and maybe someday soon it would be.

As they entered the living room, Casey left her side and went straight to the fireplace. Rebecca was not surprised, as she knew the girl was fascinated with the little wooden animals that sat there.

"Will you dust the animals for me while I dust the mantle?" Rebecca smiled when Casey bobbed her head quickly up and down. Reaching up, she took the first one off the shelf and handed it to Casey. "Here's Mr. Rabbit. Your Uncle Jake made these, you know."

Rebecca watched the child examine the bunny rabbit she held in her hands. It seemed to be her favorite, and she carefully rubbed the dust cloth over the rabbit's head. The wistful look in the child's eyes told Rebecca that Casey wished it were hers.

"He looks like he might wiggle his nose any minute, doesn't he?" Casey nodded and continued to rub the little rabbit. Her fingers ran down its sides as if she were petting a real rabbit.

"Your Uncle Jake gave me one of an apple blossom several years ago for my birthday. I can show it to you later if you like." The little girl was too absorbed in the animal to even look at her.

Rebecca decided then and there that she'd ask Jake if they could give Casey the little rabbit. She didn't think he would mind. Casey was obviously fascinated with the rabbit and had been since she'd first seen it.

It took the rest of the morning to clean the living room, but by lunchtime everything was vacuumed and dusted. It took her twice as long to get things done with Casey's help, but she enjoyed the time they spent together. Rebecca firmly believed that Casey needed to feel like she belonged here and wasn't just a visitor.

The back door slammed just as they finished putting away their cleaning supplies in the kitchen closet. They both turned and watched Jake stamp the snow off his boots while he removed his scarf and coat and hung them on a hook just inside the door.

"It's cold out there today. We might get a bit more snow." Jake stomped into the kitchen and headed straight for the coffeepot.

He glanced at them and smiled. Then he started to chuckle. The more he looked the more he laughed, until he was bent over with his hands on his legs and his whole body shaking.

Rebecca put her hands on her hips and gave him a mock glare. "What are you laughing at?" She knew they both looked like dirty little urchins with their hair tucked behind bandannas, aprons covering their jeans and shirts, and dirty smudges on their cheeks. Casey looked adorable with the too big apron that seemed more like a long dress even though it had been folded and tied so she wouldn't trip up in it.

She tried to look stern, but secretly she was glad. Most of the time, Jake seemed almost as solemn as Casey and Rebecca was ridiculously pleased whenever she got a smile out of either one of them, let alone a laugh.

"You two looked like you just crawled out of the rag bag." Still chuckling, he straightened and turned to Casey. "Been cleaning this morning, have you?"

Casey nodded and then hopped up and down in front of him. She pointed to the living room and then jumped up and down again.

Rebecca took pity on the quizzical look on his face. "Casey dusted the little rabbit until his coat was nice and shiny. Didn't you, honey?" She tried to wipe a smudge from the girl's cheek as she spoke.

"I'll bet you did a good job too." Jake looked at his niece with approval and the little girl shone with pride.

She held out her hand to Casey. "Come on, honey, we'll go get cleaned up while Uncle Jake starts making sandwiches for lunch. Maybe he'll make us some ham and cheese ones." She heard Jake start laughing again as they headed upstairs to the bathroom to clean themselves up.

A minute later, she was chuckling herself. "What a sight we are." It was a good thing she had a sense of humor, she thought wryly. How many other women would appreciate the fact that their husband got a good laugh because they looked like they spent the morning in a chimney? Oh well, he'd known she was no raving beauty when he married her, but she had made him laugh and somehow she knew that was more important than physical beauty would ever be.

It didn't take them long to scrub and rinse their faces and hands, brush their hair, and then scurry back downstairs to the kitchen. They were quick but their shirts had dark spots where they had splashed each other in their haste.

Jake had a plate with ham and cheese sandwiches and chips set at each place. He took one look at them and shook his head. But he made no comment about their damp attire. Rebecca poured milk while Jake settled Casey in her chair, and soon they were all munching hungrily on sandwiches and crunching noisily on chips.

"How was your morning?" she asked, hoping he would volunteer more than his usual "okay" and was actually surprised when he did.

"It was a good morning's work." Jake answered between bites of his sandwich. "I should be ready to leave on schedule in a week or so."

Rebecca's glass of milk fell back to the table with a "thunk." Milk lapped over the side of her glass and onto her hand, but she barely even noticed. "What do you mean *leave*? Where exactly are you going?"

He seemed uncomfortable as he spoke, as if he wasn't used to explaining himself to anyone. "I've got to go to Augusta for a few days and probably to Auburn and Lewiston as well." He stopped, as if in thought. "I may go to Portland too." He picked up his sandwich and shoved it into his mouth, all his attention focused on eating.

She waited for him to continue, but after about a minute it was clear that, as far as he was concerned, he was finished. She tried desperately to hang on to her waning patience. "Why exactly do you have to go to Augusta?"

"I've got some business there."

Rebecca's grip on her temper slipped a notch with his nonchalant reply. She clenched her jaw to keep from yelling at him and managed what she hoped was a fairly calm tone. "If it's not too much trouble I'd like to know what business and for how long." Her hands were white as they fisted in her lap while she waited for his reply.

"We can talk about it later." He abruptly stood up. "I've got to get back to work." He shot a pointed glance at Casey and then back at Rebecca.

Rebecca saw how Casey was watching her aunt and uncle with fear in her eyes. "Later," she answered. She looked away from her husband before he saw the hurt in her eyes. Jake's boots thumped across the kitchen floor and then he was gone, as the back door slammed shut behind him.

She mustered a smile, hoping it looked more real than it felt, as she turned towards Casey. "How about after we clean up the dishes we make chocolate chip cookies?"

Casey appeared hesitant, eyes downcast, but she gave one quick nod.

The rest of the day passed quietly. They made chocolate chip cookies, but Casey didn't seem to take much joy in the stirring of the batter and the rolling of the cookies for the pan. Instead, she seemed determined. Rebecca knew just how she felt. She tried to keep them both busy and to put her mind to other things.

Later the child sat at the table in the sewing room and colored pictures in her new Disney coloring book. Rebecca was disturbed by the intensity with which Casey colored, cracking several of her crayons because she was pressing so hard.

Keeping one eye on Casey, Rebecca worked on a set of curtains that had been special-ordered and had to be finished in two days. She would rather have gone to bed and pulled the covers over her, but she persevered and made headway on her sewing.

Suppertime came and the two of them picked at a chicken casserole and fresh bread. Rebecca kept looking at the clock, but time went by and there was no sign of Jake. She debated going out to look for him but decided he'd be back when he was ready.

When the dishes were washed and put away, she and Casey played games at the table. She knew the child was upset, because she kept going to the back window to look out into the darkness. Each time Casey came back to the table, she was more withdrawn. Bath time, which was usually a fun time for them both, was a chore to get through.

By the time bedtime came, Casey was obviously very upset and Rebecca's temper was about to burst. Jake might not care about her feelings, but that was no reason to hurt Casey. The little girl had refused to eat the cookies they had made. She had kept staring at Jake's chair until Rebecca realized that unless Jake was there Casey would not eat them. Casey had even made an extra large cookie especially for him. She had shaped the dough on the pan and watched through the oven door all the while it had been baking and had smiled when they had lifted it onto the cooling rack.

"It's okay, honey," Rebecca soothed Casey after reading her a second bedtime story. Usually she loved the stories of *Cinderella* and *Sleeping Beauty*, but tonight neither held the child's attention.

"Uncle Jake is just working. He'll come and kiss you before he goes to bed." She brushed Casey's hair with her hand.

"I can kiss you now."

Rebecca jerked around at the sound of his voice and was surprised to see him standing in the doorway. He'd been so quiet, she hadn't heard him come in. Sometimes he was quieter than Casey was.

Bending down, she gave Casey a kiss and moved aside so he could finish tucking the little girl into bed.

"Is that big cookie on the kitchen counter for me?" he asked as he folded the covers under Casey's chin.

Her eyes were so much like his, Rebecca thought as he smoothed Casey's hair away from her face. His big hands were so gentle.

Casey nodded shyly as he smiled at her. "I think I'll eat it before I go to bed it looks so good. Thanks for making it for me."

Casey sat up in bed, threw her arms around him, and then burst into tears.

Jake seemed stunned and horrified when her small arms shot out and grabbed on to him. No sound came from her, but her little body shook as she cried.

He had such a bewildered expression on his face that Rebecca took pity on him. "I think she thought you were mad at us," she whispered softly. "You didn't come in for supper." She knew it wasn't his fault that he wasn't used to sharing his plans with others. But he had a family now and it was time he adjusted some of his thinking no matter how hard it might be for him.

Jake held his niece tight and soothed her as best he could. He reassured her everything was all right, saying it over and over again until her little body went limp in his arms. Even then he seemed loath to release her.

But, eventually, he gently laid her back in her bed and tucked the covers in around her. Rebecca gave his arm a reassuring squeeze as he stood there watching the little tear-stained face that had become so dear to them both. His eyes never left Casey's sleeping form.

"I'll go put on coffee. Come down when you're ready and we'll talk." She left the room and slowly walked down the stairs to the kitchen. She knew he needed time to compose himself.

Almost ten minutes had passed before Jake finally joined her. He had obviously taken the time to get a quick wash as the front of his hair was damp, but had been combed into a semblance of neatness. She poured two mugs of coffee and set them on the table. With nothing left to do, she sat and waited and waited.

She sighed and opened her mouth to speak, not sure which words would spill out.

"I'm sorry about lunchtime," he stated abruptly.

Rebecca closed her mouth in a hurry. She was surprised by the apology, but she said nothing, waiting to see what else he had to say.

Jake ran his hand through his hair in obvious agitation. "I've never told anyone around here about this, and I don't want anyone else to know." He fixed a glare on her, presumably so she'd know he was serious.

"You should realize by now that anything you say is safe with me," she replied with quiet dignity.

He sighed deeply, "I know that, Rebecca, but it's hard to tell this." He glanced down at the table and then back at her. "You know those little animals in the living room?"

"Yes," she replied tentatively, not sure what he wanted her to say about them.

"I always fooled around with carving as a kid, but after I came back to the farm I started doing it more seriously. It was a way to pass the long winter months. Anyhow, I went to visit a buddy of mine in Augusta about five years ago. John had just gotten married so I took a carving I'd done as a present. It was only two little squirrels on a branch, but they loved it. His wife, Angie, wanted to know who the artist was." Jake glanced up at her and she nodded encouragingly. He continued.

"She has a friend, a lady named Evelyn Adams, who runs a gallery in Augusta. Angie showed her the carving and she wanted to see more. She liked them and since then I've been taking all my work to her in the spring and she sells them in her galleries all summer long." He sat up straighter in the chair and nonchalantly took a sip of coffee. His emotionless gaze never left her face.

Rebecca was stunned. She didn't know what to say. She couldn't believe Jake kept a secret like this! This was astonishing. It was amazing.

She shot out of her chair and threw herself onto his lap in a flash, wrapping her arms around him and hugging him.

"That's wonderful, Jake. Of course I always knew your carvings were special." She gently put her hands on the sides of his face. "But why did you keep it a secret, especially from me?" She couldn't hide the fact that as pleased as she was for him she was also hurt.

"Well heck, Rebecca, I'm not an artist, I'm a farmer." He wrapped his arm around her back to help support her. "I just do this for fun." He shook his head, his face a picture of disbelief. "You won't believe what people are paying for this stuff."

She was shocked as she finally understood. Jake was actually insecure about his status as an artist. "I'm sure this Evelyn Adams knows what she's doing and if she thinks your work is worth a lot of money, then it is." She hugged him close as she sought to reassure him.

"But my large pieces are selling for several thousand each. Even the little ones like the ones in the living room are a hundred or more."

"Oh my," she gasped in surprise. "I guess I'd better not ask for the little rabbit."

Jake looked perplexed at the sudden change in subject. "What does the rabbit have to do with anything?"

Rebecca bit her lip, suddenly nervous. "I've been letting Casey dust them when we clean the living room. She's very taken with them, but she's careful with them," she added quickly.

"It's okay for her to play with them." He shrugged. "They're just carved toys."

"No they're not. They're works of art." The words just stumbled out of her mouth. "I had no idea they were so expensive. Good heavens, the little flower you did for me must be worth several hundred dollars. Oh, Jake, I had no idea. I mean, I treasure it because you made it for me, but I didn't know it was worth money." She hardly knew what she was saying, he had her so flustered.

Jake started to laugh. She felt his shoulders start to shake and she soon found herself laughing as well, even as she gave him a playful swat and admonished him to stop. That, of course, made him laugh even harder and it was a while before he regained control.

"Why didn't you tell me?" She couldn't resist running her hands up and down his arms as she spoke. She loved touching him and having him right in front of her was too much temptation to resist.

"I guess because I feel like a bit of a fraud." He seemed to search for the right words. "I enjoy doing the carvings. It's not hard work, but pleasure for me. My father always looked at it as a hobby, certainly not as a way to make a living. The funny thing is I can make almost as much on the carvings in a year as I can on the farm." He seemed bewildered by how much money people were willing to pay for his work.

Rebecca gazed at the face she loved more than any other. He was so unaware of his own talents and appeal. "So you deliver your carvings every year in the spring?"

"Yeah. I take a few days and get all the paperwork done and pick up the check for the last year's work. I get her to pay me in one big check a year, then I spend a day or so shopping for anything I need that I can't get in Jamesville. Last year I bought a new truck even though the old one was still in pretty good shape."

"That's when you sold your old truck to Dani."

"Exactly." He continued, "Evelyn's got a new gallery opened in Lewiston and another one in Portland. I'm going to stop there for a day, check it out, and leave whatever pieces we decide on. I'll only be gone a few days." He held her hands tight in his. "Are you mad at me?"

She gave his hands a squeeze. "Not anymore. And I wouldn't have been angry in the first place if you'd just explained. I'm proud of you, and I understand if you have to go away on business. But," she added, "I will be mad if you don't show me your carvings before you take them to this Evelyn Adams."

Jake was grinning like a fool, but couldn't seem to stop. "You really want to see them?"

Rebecca nodded. "And Casey will want to see them too. She's in love with the little rabbit carving. I was going to ask you if she could have it before I realized how valuable it is."

He sobered immediately. "Of course, she can have it. I'll give it to her tomorrow." He hurried on before she could interrupt him. "Its only value to me is in her joy of it. I can make another one if anything happens to it. Let her play with it and enjoy it. That's what it's meant for. That's why I started carving them when I was a kid."

"Oh, Jake!" He constantly surprised her by how sensitive he was sometimes. It gave her great hope for the future. She threw her arms around his neck and kissed him.

It started out as an innocent thank you kiss, but quickly turned into a raging fire of longing. Jake rose from the chair with her wrapped tightly in his arms. He stopped only long enough to turn off the coffeepot and flick off the light switch. He carried her up the stairs and into their room. It was a long time before either one of them slept.

Chapter Eleven

The first week in April showed definite signs of spring. All over Jamesville and into the countryside, as well as on the Tanners' farm, the snow finally melted and the days were warming. The spring bulbs were poking their heads above the cold barren ground and it was only a matter of time before they bloomed in a rainbow of colors. Rebecca inhaled deeply as she walked to the barn, enjoying the crisp smell in the air. She absentmindedly adjusted the wicker basket she was carrying as she took in the sights and smells of the day. She loved this time of year. It was a time for new beginnings and new growth. It was a time of hope.

And she was hopeful. She felt that they were closer since the night he told her about his other career. She still couldn't believe that he found it embarrassing to be called an artist. When she'd seen the rest of his work, she'd been in awe of his talent. He had certainly improved since he'd done the carvings in the living room. They were beautiful, but his new work was breathtaking.

Moose, wolves, ducks, squirrels, and a variety of other animals and birds all came alive in his work. Every detail was remarkably precise. You could almost hear the wolf howl and the squirrels chatter. She shook her head. He truly had no idea how amazing his talent was.

She quickened her step as she neared the barn, shifting the basket yet again so she wouldn't drop it. Casey and Jake were inside, carefully wrapping and packing his work into boxes. He was leaving tomorrow, but only for a few days. Not so long at all, she told herself, but she knew in her heart that she would miss him terribly.

As she climbed the stairs to the workshop, she heard Jake's voice as he chatted to Casey. He was so good with her. Casey had been thrilled when Jake had given her the little rabbit for her very own. Ever since then, she had carried it everywhere with her during the day and set it on her nightstand next to her bed at night. She was never without it.

"Anybody ready for a cookie break?"

Jake looked up from the box he was closing. "I sure could use something. How about you?" He reached out and tousled Casey's mop of black curls. He laughed as she nodded with great enthusiasm.

Rebecca set the basket on top of the wooden workbench and unpacked a thermos of lemonade, glasses, napkins, and a large container filled with chocolate chip cookies she had just taken out of the oven. Jake set two chairs next to the bench and lifted Casey onto his lap. She busied herself pouring glasses of lemonade and handing out cookies and napkins. The room was silent as they all ate and drank greedily. It had been a busy morning for everyone, and cookies hit the spot.

"Is the packing almost done?" Rebecca sat back in her chair, feeling replete after her snack. She licked some melted chocolate from her fingers, just like a kid, but in her mind, you didn't waste good chocolate.

Jake swallowed and his eyes seemed fixed on her fingers. He cleared his throat. "Yeah. All that's left is to load the boxes in the truck. I'll carry them downstairs later and put them by the door so they'll be quick to load in the morning."

He set Casey on her feet and they watched as she wandered off in the corner to play with her little wooden rabbit. Sitting on the floor, she moved the rabbit to and fro as if she was making up a story in her head and having the rabbit perform all the action.

"You'll be all right while I'm gone?" Jake still watched Casey as he spoke.

"Of course, we'll be fine. What could go wrong? Besides, you'll only be gone a couple of days, not weeks." She put on a brave face, smiling even though her heart hurt. It was silly to miss him already, when he hadn't even left yet.

"You could at least pretend you'll miss me," he added wryly. "You're hard on a man's ego, Rebecca."

"Of course I'll miss you." She reached out her hand and touched his face. "I'm trying to be brave, but you have to miss me too."

Jake reached out and lifted her out of her chair and into his lap. "I'll miss you. I'll miss both of you," he added softly as he settled back in his chair.

Sighing, she snuggled close to Jake. She truly didn't know how much he would miss her. Sometimes she felt as if he cared about her, and other times she felt as if he cared because she made his life easier and took care of Casey.

No. That wasn't fair to Jake, she thought. He was trying to make this marriage work. She had to stop expecting too much too fast. But she really was going to miss him. She snuggled closer to him and watched Casey play. It was only for a few days. She and Casey would be just fine.

Jake was up and away early the next morning. As she stood in the back doorway and watched him drive away, Rebecca was torn between smiling and crying, so she did both. She couldn't help smiling as she thought about last night. Jake had been insatiable. Come to think of it, so had she. He couldn't seem to get enough of her and had spent several hours touching her, kissing her, lingering over her body as if he would never have enough. She knew he was going to miss her while he was gone and that made her feel good. She would miss him too and that was making her weepy.

She felt a tug on her hand and looked down at Casey. "I'm okay, sweetie, I'm just going to miss your Uncle Jake. But," she continued cheerfully. "He'll be home before we know it." She bent down and kissed the top of the child's head as she led her into the kitchen. "Maybe we'll go to town today ourselves. We need to do some grocery shopping and we can have lunch out while we're there. Kind of a girls-only day. What do you think?" Casey smiled and nodded, making her curls bounce with the motion.

Rebecca was beginning to feel better already. The days would pass quickly, and while Jake was gone, there was something she had to do— something she needed to buy at the drugstore. A little kit that would tell her if her suspicion was correct. She thought she might be pregnant, maybe about six weeks along, but she wanted to be sure before she checked with her doctor. If she was right, she'd have a great big surprise for her husband when he got home. She patted her tummy lovingly as she went back into the kitchen to make a grocery list.

The little stick was the right color. Rebecca looked at the box and checked to make sure. She looked at the stick once more and then checked the box again. She wrapped her arms around herself, tight. She wanted to scream. She wanted to dance. She was pregnant with Jake's baby.

She stared out the bathroom window at the world beyond. It was the same. The sky was blue, the sun was shining, the crows were cawing and swooping through the air. It was amazing how the world outside the window looked ordinary when the world inside had just changed in such an amazing way.

It was like a dream come true. She was married to the man she loved and their marriage, while not perfect, was progressing at a rate that gave her great hope for the future. She had a little girl she loved with all her heart, and now this. A baby. She could hardly believe how much her life had changed in a few short months.

They hadn't discussed having children right away, but Jake hadn't used any protection and she knew he wanted children. She didn't care if it was a boy or a girl as long as it was a healthy baby. She knew that he would feel the same.

There was so much to do and to think about, she couldn't wrap her head around it all. She would have to make an appointment with her doctor. She hoped she got one before Jake got home. They'd tell Casey about it together so they could reassure her and make her understand that she was going to have a cousin of her very own.

She bit her bottom lip, worrying, as she thought about Casey. They'd had such a wonderful day yesterday. They had grocery shopped, done some window-shopping, and stopped into Jessie's for lunch. Casey had been happy and contented until bedtime. She had obviously missed her Uncle Jake when it was time to get tucked into bed. Rebecca had again explained to her that her Jake was only gone for a few days and would be home soon. It had taken a lot of comforting and kisses before she had finally drifted into a restless sleep.

Rebecca supposed that it was only normal for a child who had been through as much upheaval as Casey had to dread any changes in what had become a cherished bedtime routine. Jake should have called, but he hadn't, and she had suddenly realized that she didn't even know what hotel he was staying at. She knew she could reach him through Evelyn Adam's art gallery, if she had to, but she would only do so in an emergency.

Still, she wished he had called, even just to say goodnight to Casey. If she was being honest, and she tried to be, she wished he had called just so she could have heard his gruff voice whisper good night to her. She was as bad as Casey and hadn't slept well because her own bedtime routine, which now included Jake, had been interrupted.

The patter of little feet made her toss the pregnancy test in the garbage and leave the bathroom. Sure enough Casey stood in the bedroom doorway looking for her. "Good morning, sweetie. Did you sleep well?" She was surprised her voice sounded normal when she felt anything but normal.

Casey gave her a sleepy smile and scampered over with her arms held out. Rebecca scooped up the little girl and gave her a hug. "Were you feeling lonely, honey?" She felt the tentative nod against her shoulder.

"How about after breakfast we go outside and size up where we want to put our garden this year? This afternoon we can work in the sewing room and I can finish that dress I'm making for Mrs. Greer's granddaughter. We can fry some chicken for supper and maybe even make some apple tarts for dessert. Would you like that?" Rebecca figured it was better if she kept Casey busy. Come to think of it, it was probably best for her as well. It would keep them from missing Jake too much.

Casey wiggled until Rebecca put her down. She watched as the little girl turned, ran out the door and down the hall to her room to get dressed.

She wished she had more time to savor her news, but she knew Casey would dress quickly. Turning to the closet she pulled out a clean pair of jeans and smiled slightly as she wondered how much longer they would fit her. She had a ton of questions and knew that one of her chores for today was making an appointment with her doctor so she could get them answered. The sound of small feet stomping down the stairs made her finish dressing. She would make them a big breakfast. After all she was now eating for two.

It was a busy morning, and by the time they planned their garden, it was lunchtime. They had stomped around the outside of the house all morning, measuring garden plots and planning what flowers they would put where. Casey had helped her decide on flowers by pointing to pictures in a seed catalog as they had poured over their choices. Rebecca had managed to steer the girl towards hearty, inexpensive flowers like sunflowers, daisies, violets, and forget-me-nots. By summer, the garden would be awash with color. She grinned as she wondered how Jake was going to react to all those flowers.

The afternoon in the sewing room had stretched out until suppertime. It was hard to make progress when she had to stop every few minutes and play dolls with Casey or to admire a picture she had colored. Rebecca didn't mind, though, and in fact enjoyed it, but it made her consider how much work she could actually take in now that she had Casey to look after and a baby on the way. It was something she had to think about.

By the time they made the fruit tarts, ate supper and cleared away, it was bedtime for Casey. It was worse than the night before. Casey had fretted endlessly and cried herself to sleep while Rebecca had watched, helpless to comfort the child in any way except with her presence. She kept telling Casey that her Uncle Jake might be back tomorrow. Cold comfort for a child.

By the time the child had drifted off to sleep, Rebecca was exhausted and more than ready for bed herself. Like the night before, she tossed and turned, wondering where Jake was. One minute, she was angry that he hadn't called and the next, she was concerned. Wrapping her arms around his pillow, she hugged it tight. She missed him and wanted to hear his voice. Eventually, she fell into a restless sleep.

Chapter Twelve

After tossing and turning all night long, Rebecca woke up feeling more tired than before she went to bed. She was lying there, staring aimlessly at the ceiling, trying to get the energy to drag herself up, when the first wave of nausea hit her. Flinging back the covers, she scrambled to the bathroom, hoping to make it in time. Falling to her knees, she lost what looked like most of last night's supper. "Oh great," she muttered as she grasped the sides of the porcelain bowl for support.

Then it struck her. She'd just had her first bout of morning sickness. Suddenly, her pregnancy was real to her in a way that it hadn't been yesterday. There was a whole new little person inside of her, waiting to be born. She rose unsteadily to her feet, grinning like a fool and kept smiling even as she brushed her teeth and rinsed her mouth. Not an easy feat.

A quick shower had her feeling better in no time at all. She was suddenly energized. She made the bed, got dressed, hurried downstairs and was whipping up a batch of pancakes when Casey entered the kitchen with her doll in tow.

Breakfast was a quick affair, or as quick as it could be with a four-year-old. Casey ate slowly, chewing every small piece of food about twenty times. Rebecca passed the time planning and decided that if she finished sewing the dress she was working on this morning, she and Casey would have the whole afternoon to do something special.

She was so caught up in her plans that she didn't notice Casey was less active than usual, almost withdrawn, as she ate her breakfast. And when she settled in to play quietly in the sewing room an hour later, Rebecca assumed the child was merely tired and missing her Uncle Jake. Taking advantage of the uninterrupted time, Rebecca put her head down and sewed, hoping to get finished before she got bored with her play.

"It's finally finished. What do you think?" Rebecca held the peach-colored dress up in front of her and looked toward Casey to get her opinion. The coloring book was lying open on the floor with crayons scattered all around it, but there was no sign of the little girl.

Rebecca frowned as she got up from the sewing machine and laid the dress across the chair. She hadn't heard Casey leave the room.

"Casey. Where are you sweetie?" Rebecca checked the kitchen first. No Casey. She went upstairs. Maybe she had wanted to get one of her other toys to play with. Rebecca looked in Casey's room. No Casey.

"Stay calm. Stay calm," she repeated as she hurried to check her own room. She rushed from room to room calling Casey's name. Nothing. Not a sign or a sound. She raced down the stairs and checked the living room and the office. Nothing.

That's when she noticed the back door was open a crack.

"Oh my Lord."

She raced to the door, jerked it open, and looked out, hoping to see Casey playing in the yard. She pulled on her shoes, grabbed her coat, and rushed out the door, calling as she went. "Casey! Casey! Come on out, sweetie!"

She ran around the house. When that earned her nothing, she ran to the barn. Maybe Casey had gone out to Jake's workshop to play. Lord, she hoped not. There were tools out there that Casey could hurt herself with. "Don't even think it," she chastised herself.

She would find the child there and everything would be fine. She would have a long talk to Casey about wandering off and that would be the end of it. Praying that was so, she raced up the steps to the workshop. She burst into the room and searched everywhere. Again, no sign of Casey.

She raced back down the stairs and checked everywhere in the barn, calling as she went. "Casey! Casey!"

By the time she had searched the barn, she was in tears. She couldn't find her little girl anywhere. Whirling around in a circle in the middle of the yard, she called Casey's name over and over.

Dizziness and nausea came out of nowhere. She fell to her knees and dropped her head to the ground. It was then she realized how hard she was breathing. She took several deep breaths. She had to get control of herself. This was no time to panic. She needed help. Rebecca struggled to her feet and headed to the house.

Sheriff Albert Tucker arrived ten minutes later, and Rebecca was never so glad to see anyone in her whole life. He was a big, no-nonsense man in his early fifties. His shrewd brown eyes had crow's feet radiating from the corners, and his nose had obviously been broken on more than one occasion. His mouth could firm into a stern line or smile depending on the circumstances. It was an endearingly homely face, but more importantly, Sheriff Tucker had the tenacity of a bulldog. He would help her find Casey.

His mouth was not smiling as he got out of his patrol car. "I got your message. How long has she been missing?"

"I'm not sure. I know that sounds awful. How could I not know?" She knew she sounded half-hysterical, but couldn't seem to control herself. What kind of a mother was she that she didn't know how long her child was missing? Because Casey was her child. She didn't feel like an aunt. She felt like a mother. A mother who had lost her child.

"Calm down, Rebecca. I've raised three kids of my own and I know how easy it is to lose track of them." He offered her a reassuring smile.

"She's quiet. I mean, she doesn't talk, but she's a very quiet child. She plays in the sewing room with me while I work. She colors or reads or plays with her doll." Rebecca paused for a breath.

"I finished sewing a dress about a half an hour or so ago, I guess. I looked up to show her and she wasn't there. I searched the house first, thinking she must have gone to her room for a new toy or something, but she wasn't there. I've been through the house and the barn," her voice rose in panic. "And I can't find her."

She looked at the sheriff, barely able to see him as tears filled her eyes. "I looked everywhere and I couldn't find her. You've got to help me find her!" She burst into tears, unable to hold back any longer. Rebecca turned away from the sheriff, ashamed of her outburst.

Sheriff Tucker laid a reassuring hand on her shoulder. "We'll find her, Rebecca. She probably wandered off to explore and got lost." Rebecca could tell by the look on his face that he hoped that was all it was.

He turned as another official vehicle pulled in. "Let me talk to my men. We'll have a search going in no time." Leaving her alone, he strode towards the two men getting out of the car.

Five hours later, the search had grown. Word travels fast in a small town, and within a few hours, the search parties had grown to include neighbors and concerned townspeople. Burke Black and Shamus O'Rourke had arrived within an hour of hearing about Casey going missing and they called their friends, and on it went until there were now about fifty men and women searching for the little girl.

Rebecca was back at the house again. The sheriff had wanted her to stay close to the farmhouse in case Casey wandered home on her own. Rebecca had placed a frantic call to the gallery in Augusta only to be told that, as far as they knew, Jake was on his way home. She wanted him home. Now. She knew it was irrational, but she felt that if Jake were there, everything would be all right. He would find Casey.

She wandered around the kitchen, absently noting that the table and counters were covered with plates of sandwiches, pies, and cookies. A huge coffee urn had been set up on the counter with a stack of paper cups next to it, ready when anyone wanted some. Many of the women, who couldn't come themselves because they had families of their own to look after, had sent food along with their men. Dani, who was due to have her baby any day now, was unable to participate in the actual search. Instead, she had sent a huge coffee urn and paper cups, along with her husband, Burke.

The sight and smell of all that food and coffee made her stomach churn, so she turned her back on it. She knew the searchers would be hungry soon, but she couldn't eat. Not with Casey out there somewhere, alone, maybe cold and hungry. The thought was almost more than she could bear. She swallowed hard to keep the nausea at bay.

Her head snapped up as she heard a vehicle pull up behind the house. Maybe someone had found Casey. She rushed to the back door and flung it open. It wasn't Casey, but it was the next best thing. Jake was home! Jake would find her. She raced out the door towards him, her arms outstretched to greet him. She needed him to hold her, if only for a minute.

Jake brought the truck to a screeching halt as she ran out the back door. She knew that the sight of so many police vehicles and other trucks would have alerted him to the fact something was wrong.

Jumping out of the truck, he met her halfway. He caught her as she flung herself in his arms.

"Oh Jake, Oh Jake." She couldn't seem to make herself say anything more.

Jake held her tight, as if to assure himself that she was okay, but she couldn't stop shaking. He lifted her into his arms, carried her into the kitchen and set her down on a kitchen chair.

He grasped her shoulders and shook her lightly. "What's wrong, honey? Tell me what's wrong."

"It's Casey," Rebecca sobbed. "She's missing."

He looked at her as if he couldn't understand what she was saying. "What do you mean she's missing?"

"One minute she was with me in the sewing room, and the next she was gone. I looked everywhere, but I couldn't find her. I called Sheriff Tucker and they've been looking all afternoon." She knew she was talking way too fast, but she had to tell him everything so he could find Casey.

"What do you mean, one minute she was gone? Weren't you watching her?" Jake growled. His lips thinned and his eyes glittered with anger.

Rebecca was taken aback by his outburst. "Of course I was watching her. She was with me in the sewing room." She was sure she had made that fact very clear.

"In the damn sewing room. So what you're saying is that your sewing was more important than Casey." He glared at her.

"That's not so, Jake." She had to make him understand.

"All I know is that the only reason I married you, Rebecca, was to take care of Casey. And you couldn't do it for me. That was the only job you needed." Jake's hands slipped from her shoulders as he stepped away, a pained look on his face. "That little girl is the most important thing. How could you forget that for a second? She's the reason you're here." He turned away from her, as if he couldn't stand to look at her any longer.

Rebecca was stunned by Jake's attack. Families pulled together at times like this. Didn't they? But they weren't really a family, she thought as she stared at Jake's rigid back. That was merely a fantasy she had played out in her own head. The pain inside her now was almost crippling, but she shoved it to the back of her mind. Casey was missing. She had a child to find. When she returned Casey to Jake, she'd give in to her own heartache and pain.

"I'm going to join the search." Storming out the back door, Jake headed towards the orchards. He never looked back, not realizing the devastation he had left behind him.

She knew that all his energy was focused on finding Casey. There wasn't much daylight left.

Rebecca sat alone at the kitchen table, watching the determination in his stride as he walked away from the house. Away from her. She felt unable to move. She was numb from head to toe, and somewhere in her mind she knew that was a good thing. She couldn't afford to feel right now. It would destroy her. Later, when there was time, she would lick her wounds in private. She would have to come to terms with what Jake really thought of her. She shuddered and shoved that thought away. Later, not now.

She pulled herself up and steadied herself against the table as nausea and dizziness threatened to overcome her. With firm resolve, she straightened her legs and took a deep breath. Her boots thumped across the floor as she walked out the door to rejoin the search for her little girl.

Chapter Thirteen

After checking with the sheriff, Jake began his own search of the apple orchards. There were acres of trees, and although they were still barren, there were plenty of places for a little girl to hide. Some of the men had already searched the orchards, but it occurred to Jake that Casey might actually hide from her rescuers. She was alone, afraid, and she wouldn't know any of these strangers who were calling for her. He didn't want to think of the alternative, that maybe she was hurt and couldn't get to the searchers when they called her name. Casey couldn't call for help if she was hurt or in trouble.

His hands clenched and unclenched as he walked the path between the trees, calling out to her. He wanted to run, but forced himself to be slow and thorough. The throbbing in his head matched the pain in his heart. He knew his anger at Rebecca was unreasonable, but he felt it all the same. How could she lose their little girl? How could she not have known Casey had left the room?

A thought flashed in his head and he stopped cold. "I should have been here," he muttered as he turned in a full circle, squinting against the coming darkness, hoping to see some sign of Casey. If he hadn't been away none of this might have happened. He shook himself and continued down the path. He didn't want to examine that thought too closely at the moment. Quickening his step, he pushed his anger aside. Right now he had to concentrate on finding Casey. Everything else could wait.

As his boots crushed the dead leaves and grass beneath his feet, his eyes kept scanning back and forth among the trees. She had to be here.

He remembered himself as a kid. He and Hank would play and hide among the trees, pretending they were explorers of a strange new world. They would run up and down the paths and hide in the low branches of the apple trees. If he listened hard enough, he could almost hear the echo of their laughter. Lord, that seemed like such a long time ago. When had they drifted apart? Jake sometimes wondered if he'd ever known his brother at all. Now it was too late, they would never have the chance to know if they could have formed some kind of friendship. Maybe, if he'd tried harder.

He shook off the melancholy thoughts and kept calling. He had to concentrate on Casey. She was his family now.

"Casey, its Uncle Jake. Come on out, honey. It's time to go in for supper." He tried to keep the fear and anger out of his voice, afraid she wouldn't come to him if she thought he was upset with her.

The sun was sinking fast. It would be colder soon and dark. He walked a little faster. "Casey! Where are you, honey? It's time to go home."

Despair welled up inside him as a shiver moved down his spine. They weren't going to find her in time. Soon it would be too dark to search and they would have to call it off until morning. His eyes moved methodically from side to side, desperate not to miss any movement, any sign. He couldn't bear to think of his little girl alone in the dark, scared and hungry and cold.

"Casey!" He called her name again in desperation.

He swung around. Was that a sound? Had he heard something? He listened for a long moment and tried again. "Casey honey, it's Uncle Jake. It's time to go home now."

At first he wasn't sure he believed his ears. Surely it was his imagination or a whisper on the wind. Just as he was about to call out, he heard it again.

"Uncle Jake."

Spinning toward the sound, he saw two little eyes and a mop of black curls peeking out from behind the trunk of the gnarled old apple tree. He didn't remember moving, but suddenly she was in his arms. She was real and she was okay. Jake held her as tightly as he dared, afraid that if he let himself go he might squeeze her too hard. His eyes filled with moisture and he blinked quickly to try and beat back the tears that threatened to fall. Although he wanted to hold onto her forever, he forced himself to let her go.

He gently unlocked his arms from around her, held her away from him and examined her from head to toe, running his hands gently over her small limbs, testing for injuries. Reassuring himself that she really was all right, he pulled her back into his arms again and hugged her. She was safe in his arms and he didn't know if he'd ever be able to let her out of his sight again.

Suddenly, he stilled as his mind began to process what had just happened. He sank to the ground and pulled Casey into his lap. He spoke softly and calmly so as not to alarm her, even though his heart was pounding so hard he could hardly hear what he was saying. "Casey, honey, did you call my name?"

She nodded solemnly and put her little hand on his cheek. "You came back, Uncle Jake," she said softly, her voice a little rough with disuse.

"Oh, baby. Oh, baby." Jake couldn't say anything else. He felt the tears on his cheeks, but he didn't care. His little girl was talking. She was talking! Her voice was soft and her words hesitant, but she was talking. He had to tell Rebecca.

He suddenly remembered why he was out here in the first place. "Why did you run away?"

She looked at him, her big green eyes serious. "I went to find you, Uncle Jake. You went away and didn't come back. I missed you. Aunt Rebecca cried." She ducked her head away from him. "I thought you wouldn't come back, like Mommy and Daddy. I wanted to find you to make Aunt Rebecca happy again. I didn't want you to go away." Her voice got stronger and grew more sure with each word she spoke.

Jake was speechless. "I wasn't gone for good, only on a trip." He tried to find a way to explain. "Your mommy and daddy are gone to heaven. They didn't want to leave you, but they got hurt in an accident."

Casey nodded. "They went away a lot, but they came back before. Mommy said if I was good while they were gone, she would come back."

Jake hugged her tighter. He still couldn't believe she was talking to him. He wasn't pleased with the way her parents had raised her. No child needed that kind of guilt. But it served no purpose to think ill of the dead, and besides, Casey was with him now. He would make sure her life from here on was a good one.

"I'll always come back to you, honey." He held her at arm's length, his expression serious as he looked at her. "We've got to go home now. Folks are worried about you.

You've got to promise not to go away like that again. Come to us if you're frightened or worried, but don't run away. You scared me and your aunt."

"I promise," her voice quivered and a tear ran down her cheek.

Jake used the tip of his finger to dry her tear, and then scrubbed his hand over his own cheeks to wipe away the emotional evidence from his face. He stood with Casey cradled in his arms. "Let's go home now, honey. There are a lot of people who are going to be happy to see you."

He shook his head in wonder. How could such a little person worm her way into his heart so fast? She was so small and fragile, yet she had survived such turmoil in her short life.

That comparison made him think of Rebecca. Maybe he'd been a little hard on her. She hadn't been a parent long. Maybe she hadn't realized how much you had to watch a little kid. She'd be so happy to see the little bundle in his arms. He shrugged off his concern. Casey was home now. The rest would work itself out later.

A crowd was gathered in the yard when he stepped out of the shadow of the orchard and into the backyard. It had gotten dark while he had been talking to Casey, and most of the searchers had reluctantly returned to the house. "I've got her," he called to the group milling around the back porch. As one they turned, and when they saw the child in his arms, they broke into cheers.

Rebecca, who had been talking with Burke about continuing the search, stopped when she heard Jake's voice. He seemed to appear out of nowhere, but when she saw the bundle in his arms, she let out a cry. He had her! He had their little girl! As she ran toward him, she didn't stop to think about how he had scorned her and walked away from her earlier. She wouldn't believe Casey was okay until she held the little girl in her arms.

Skidding to a halt, she slowly reached out to the child in his arms. "You're safe," she whispered, unaware of the tears rolling down her face.

Casey wrapped her small arms around her aunt.. "Don't cry. I'm sorry, Aunt Rebecca." The child started to cry as well.

Rebecca was stunned. "You're talking. You're actually talking." She wanted to scream it to the heavens, and she would have if she hadn't been afraid of scaring Casey. Instead, she gathered the little girl in her arms, held her and kissed the top of her head over and over.

When she found her own voice again, she spoke. "I'm glad you're safe, but please don't ever run away again. I missed you so much." She headed towards the house with Casey clutched tightly in her arms, still reeling from the fact that the child had actually talked.

By the time all the searchers had rehashed all the details of the rescue several times, eaten, and drunk their coffee, it was eight o'clock. The happy, laughing bunch of people that left was a far cry from the serious group of volunteers who had arrived several hours before. The lost child had been found and their small community and friends had weathered a potential storm. Life was good.

Sheriff Tucker shook hands with everyone as they left, thanking them again for their assistance. Official duties all but finished, he shook hands with both Jake and Rebecca. "I'm heading home now. The wife will have supper waiting for me and she'll be relieved to know that Casey is all right."

"Thank you so much for all your help." Jake stepped out onto the porch with Sheriff Tucker. Rebecca could hear the low sound of their voices through the screen door.

"No problem. That's what I'm here for." The sheriff stood with his hands on his hips looking out over the backyard. "You know, this kind of thing happens with kids now and again. You never know what ideas they get into their head. I just wish that all my missing kid cases worked out this well."

Their voices faded as the two men walked toward the sheriff's car. Jake was still standing there, staring out over the yard, when she and Burke stepped out onto the back porch a few minutes later.

Burke pulled Rebecca into his arms for a quick hug. "Dani will call you tomorrow. I think I can hold her off until then. She wanted to be here with you today."

"I know, Burke. I want to thank you for coming out so quickly. I know it was you who called the service clubs and rounded up so many folks to help, and on such short notice." Rebecca had known Dani for years, but she now counted Dani's husband, Burke, among her friends. He had helped her when she'd needed it most, and she would never forget that.

"If there's anything I can ever do for you," Jake added as he climbed the porch stairs and held out his hand to Burke.

Burke smiled as he shook Jake's hand. "Just glad I could help. You two take care." With that said, he made his way to his truck.

He limped slightly as he walked and Rebecca knew that it was an old injury that caused him problems when he was too hard on his leg. Searching through the fields and nearby woods all afternoon had to be catching up to him. Rebecca thought of Dani and knew her friend would take good care of her husband when he got home. "Tell Dani I'll call her."

Burke raised his hand and waved to let her know he heard her before he climbed in his truck and drove away. Jake and Rebecca watched until the truck taillights disappeared into the darkness. It was good to know that they had friends and neighbors to depend on when they needed them. They knew that not everyone could say that, and they were grateful that they were so blessed. Finally, with nothing else left to do, they turned and went back into the kitchen.

The emergency paramedics that had been on hand had checked out Casey and declared her perfectly healthy. She had been cold and hungry, but a hot bath and supper had taken care of that. She had stayed close to Rebecca, shy and uncertain of all the attention, but seemingly over her ordeal. Rebecca knew she would never get over the shock of losing Casey, even though she had come home safe.

It was still surprising every time she heard the child's soft little voice, but it was music to her ears. That was the silver lining in the dark cloud, she guessed.

Looking at the child she loved with all her heart, she wondered what she was going to do. Rubbing her pounding head, she sighed deeply. She couldn't think about her situation with Jake tonight. For tonight, all that mattered was that Casey was home, safe and warm.

Watching the child sitting at the kitchen table, playing with her wooden rabbit, it was hard to believe that such a quiet little girl had caused such a big uproar. "I think it's time for bed." She held out her hand and Casey nodded, slipping her hand into Rebecca's as she turned to look at her uncle. Jake nodded in understanding and they all walked up the stairs together. *Just like a family*. The thought pierced

Rebecca's heart. But after what Jake had said to her earlier, she knew he didn't see them that way at all.

Quickly tucking the child into bed, Rebecca kissed her good night. "Sleep well." Wanting to give Jake and Casey time together, she went back down to the kitchen to start clearing up the mess in the kitchen. It was easier to keep working than to stop and think. She wasn't ready to do that yet.

Chapter Fourteen

Jake settled on the edge of Casey's bed, gently stroking her soft hair. Long after she had drifted off to sleep, he still sat there. The room was bathed in the soft glow of the nightlight that they kept on all night because she was afraid of the dark. Her rag doll was securely clutched in her arms and her wooden bunny sat on the nightstand under a little yellow lamp. The rocking chair in the corner was piled with books, waiting to be read, and colored pictures filled the little child's table.

He had to keep looking at her to reassure himself that she was indeed home, safe and sound. As he watched her, he was filled with a feeling of peace and contentment. It was good to have a family. But he knew he was putting off the inevitable. He and Rebecca would have to discuss matters, no matter how much he was dreading the confrontation. Smoothing the covers around Casey's shoulders, he bent down and kissed her cheek. Creeping out of the room, he softly closed the door behind him.

Strolling down the stairs and into the kitchen, he poured himself another cup of coffee. Rebecca ignored him and continued clearing away food and dishes. He watched as she dried the last of the dishes and put them away in the cupboards. She wiped her hands on a towel and then headed towards the stairs. That's when Jake realized she was going to bed. He reached out his hand to stop her from walking out of the room.

"Rebecca, we have to talk." He was stunned when she flinched as if he had hit her.

"I'm tired and I think there's been enough said for one day, don't you?" Exhaustion showed in her face as she glanced at him and then away.

"No, I don't actually." His whole body tensed as he watched her like a hunter watches his prey. She wasn't leaving until he found out what was wrong with her.

Reluctantly, she turned and faced him. "Say what you've got to say."

Her face was pale and closed, and her arms were crossed tightly across her chest. He frowned with concern, for she looked close to dropping where she stood. "Sit down, Rebecca."

He ran his hand through his hair and sighed in frustration when she shook her head and refused to sit. "Look, I understand that you're not used to kids and maybe you weren't watching her close enough today, but you know now and this won't happen again." Jake thought he was being generous, all things considered.

"You really don't get it, do you?" Rebecca rubbed her tired eyes with one hand as she reached out and steadied herself on the back of a chair with the other. "I was watching her. If you think I'd neglect Casey on purpose, you don't think much of me, do you?"

"Of course I think a lot of you," Jake thundered. "I married you, didn't I? You're my wife."

Rebecca closed her eyes as if in pain. Her shoulders drooped and she bit her lip so hard she was drawing blood.

Before he could speak, she took a deep breath and steadied herself. She pulled herself upright and squarely faced him. "I thought I was."

"Of course you are. I was there when we got married." He was getting irritated all over again. Why was she being difficult about it all? Why couldn't she just see his point of view so they could go to bed and forget about it?

"Actually, a wife gets love, caring and respect." Her voice shook with anger and exhaustion. "I'm the woman you married to take care of your niece and be your housekeeper." She glared at him, her eyes accusing. "You don't even trust me enough to take care of Casey, to know I'd do anything to keep her from harm."

Jake's eyes snapped with anger as he jumped out of his chair. He began pacing in the kitchen, his stride as choppy as his voice. "You're more than a housekeeper, sweetheart. A housekeeper doesn't sleep with her employer."

"That's fixed easily enough." Rebecca twisted around and stalked out of the kitchen and up the stairs. He heard her footsteps as she went into their room and came out again. Her footsteps continued down the hallway and he heard a door close tight.

Jake stood in the kitchen, his feet stuck to the floor. He didn't understand women. What did she want him to say? Of course, she was his wife. Of course, he cared for her. Lord knows he cared for her. Thinking back to the moment he had pulled into the driveway this evening, his first thoughts had been for her, not Casey. Scowling, he got up from the table. How could she say he didn't care about her?

He locked up the house for the night and climbed the stairs. He looked in their room. Empty. Gazing down the hall, he saw the closed door of the guestroom and he knew the door would be locked. He wanted to beat his head against the wall to rid himself of his frustrations. He'd do it too, but he really didn't think it would help much. The only thing that would help would be her in bed with him and that just wasn't going to happen tonight.

He released a deep sigh. He'd talk to her again in the morning. They'd both be more rational then. At least, he hoped they would be. It was the only plan he had and he was too tired to think of another one. He dragged off his clothes and headed for the shower. It was going to be a long night.

A few hours later, he rolled over in bed and punched his pillow. The bed that had always suited him perfectly now felt huge and uncomfortable without Rebecca beside him. He had gotten used to her snuggling up close to him in the night, her arms reaching out to hold him and her sweet scent filling his nostrils. He took a deep breath and caught a hint of her scent from the blankets. Shifting again, he tried to get comfortable.

That was the problem with the night. All those long hours with nothing to do but think. He wasn't sure he wanted to examine the whole situation, because deep in his heart he knew he had overreacted. Knew he'd been wrong. And that wasn't something a man wanted to admit to himself.

Lying there, staring into the shadows of the room, there was plenty of time to reflect on what he'd said to Rebecca. There was also a lot of time to replay what she had said to him. Over and over again, the words rattled around in his brain, but it always came back to the same question. *Did he trust her?* The answer that sprung immediately to his lips was a unqualified, *yes. At least as much as I trust any woman.*

That last thought stopped him cold. Was that what he truly thought? When had he started believing that women couldn't be trusted? When had he stopped treating them as individual people and lumping them into a whole category of "not to be trusted"?

Jake let his thoughts drift back in time to his childhood. His mother had been a good one, except for one fact: she hated the farm. She would talk endlessly of her cousin who lived in New York, and how much fun she'd had when she'd visited her as a young woman. In fact, she had planned to move to New York herself before his father had swept her off her feet. The last part was always said with a sad little laugh. His mother would disappear into her bedroom at the end of the story and emerged a while later with reddened eyes. It was hard, as a kid, to know that your mother wasn't happy and you were the only reason she stayed. That and the fact she had belonged to a generation that believed marriage was forever, no matter how miserable you were.

He remembered her beautiful face that had hardly ever worn a smile. A face that had changed over the years as she and his father had grown apart while the kids were all they had in common.

His father had been an uncomplicated man. He was a farmer and content to be one. Although he'd loved his wife, he had never understood that her dissatisfaction with her life had nothing to do with him and more to do with circumstance. The result had been an ever-widening gap between them that neither one could bridge. His mother had poured over art books from the library and listened to classical music and opera on the radio. His father had read the *Farmer's Journal* and listen to the weather report. There had been no common ground.

It was strange to look back on your parents from an adult perspective. You saw them as people with their own hopes and dreams rather than just as your parents.

His parents had never really talked to one another. Never shared their interests or their passions. His father had never been able to talk to Jake's mother about the farm. She'd made it abundantly clear on many occasions that she wasn't interested. On the other hand, his father had never encouraged her to pursue any interests or to get a job outside the farm. His father had been of the old school, the one that believed that a man supports his wife and family.

Jake thought about how interested Rebecca was in the farm and how quick she was to support his art career. He winced as he remembered himself referring to her work as that "damned sewing room". He was ashamed of himself. She had been supportive and understanding of his work since the beginning. On the other hand, he had done no giving at all. In fact, he had been critical from the start. Why?

Was he like his father, afraid that she would leave him if she had the means to support herself? Was he trying to isolate her on the farm in order to keep her to himself?

Jake was appalled to realize that was indeed what he was trying to do and he also knew why. His mother had left the farm immediately after his father's funeral. She had taken the money from the small life insurance policy and headed to San Francisco. Now she lived in a tiny apartment and painted every day. She was starting to sell some of her work and she finally seemed happy. He got a card from her every Christmas, and she had sent a letter when she'd heard about Hank's death, but she hadn't come back. It was as if she felt she'd given up enough of her life for her kids and she was through with that part of her life.

Rebecca, on the other hand, cared deeply for him. He could tell by the way her eyes softened when she looked at him. He'd known for years that she was interested in him, but he had never pursued it until he'd needed a wife in a hurry. She also seemed to enjoy the farm and had, in fact, come out to the farm to pick apples every year as a teenager. The more he thought about it, the more he realized that she actually seemed happy here.

She never complained of being lonely and she seemed content. That was the word he was looking for. Contentment seemed to surround her like a warm blanket, and under her guidance the house that had been no more than a place to sleep and eat had become a home, a place he wanted to be.

And yet, he continued to treat her like she was going to leave at any minute. When he thought back on some of the things he had said to her, he was surprised that she was still here.

Trust her? He trusted her more than he'd ever trusted any woman. That was a lot for a man who had sworn never to trust another woman for as long as he lived. He had trusted a woman once, when he was a young man in college, and she had betrayed him.

Beverly Simpson. He rolled the name over in his mind and he found that for the first time, he could think about her without bitterness. Maybe it was because he had Rebecca now. Whatever the reason, he was glad the memory seemed to have lost its power to make him feel angry and hurt.

He had met Beverly during his first year in university where he had been studying agriculture. She was working on a marketing degree. He had literally bumped into her on campus, and while he was apologizing to her and helping her pick up her books off the floor, he had lost his heart. She was tall, blond and beautiful. Looking back now he could still admit she was beautiful, but she had ambition as well. If he'd stopped to think with his brain, instead of his hormones, he would have realized that there was no way she would have been content to be a farmer's wife. But he'd been young, stupid, and in love with a beautiful, smart woman who seemed to think he was something special. It had been heady stuff for a nineteen-year-old guy.

Reality had shattered the fantasy he had spun when his father died. Suddenly, he had to give up his studies and go home. He had a farm to run. He'd always known it was going to be his, but he had thought he would have a few more years before it actually happened. He'd always pictured his father retiring from the business. It had never occurred to him that his father could die.

Never one to run from his responsibilities, he had summoned his courage, bought a ring, and proposed to Beverly. He'd had it all figured out. She would marry him and they would live happily ever after, here on the farm.

She'd laughed in his face.

For as long as he lived he would never forget that moment. She had looked at him and laughed, asking him why on earth he thought she would give up all her plans to go live on some farm? She was headed for a junior partnership at a New York marketing firm, and nothing and no one would stop her.

Jake finally gave up trying to get comfortable in bed and got up. He padded across the floor to the window, his bare feet on the wood floor the only sound in the night. He gazed out onto the land with a certainty that this was the life he'd wanted and, if he was honest with himself, he was lucky Beverly had turned him down. If she hadn't, she would have been like his mother. But, unlike his mother, Beverly would have eventually left him and who knows if he would have been able to hold onto the farm in a divorce settlement. That was one of the reasons he'd had a prenuptial agreement drawn up for Rebecca to sign.

Rebecca. She was indeed a special lady and he was lucky to have her for a wife. He knew he was being unfair to her, but somehow, until tonight, he had never understood why. Maybe now he'd stop putting his foot in his mouth at every turn. If he'd kept his mouth shut tonight, she might be lying in bed waiting for him even now. He stopped that thought. Too much of that and he'd never get any sleep.

As he continued to stare out the window at the land he loved, he saw the stars twinkling in the sky. That's what Rebecca had done for him. She had brought some light into his lonely life. Not just light, but laughter and caring as well. She had made his life better simply by being here on a daily basis.

He knew he'd have to apologize to her. Deep in his heart he knew she would do anything to keep Casey safe. Only an idiot couldn't see how much she loved the little girl and he figured he wasn't an idiot, even if he was acting like one lately.

It had been his own insecurities, and the anger he'd directed at himself for not being here when Casey needed him, that had caused him to lash out at Rebecca like a wounded bear. A man wanted to be there to protect his family, and he had been gone. He knew that this might have happened at some other time even if he'd been here. Who knew what went on in a kid's mind? He'd had no idea that Casey had feared he wouldn't return. He had told her he would and in his own mind that was good enough. Obviously, it hadn't been enough for a scared little girl. Shaking his head, he realized he had a lot to learn about kids.

He pictured Rebecca carrying his baby and grinned. If he didn't get his marriage straightened out there was no way that image would ever become a reality. He'd like to have a child with Rebecca, maybe even two or three. Just by admitting that to himself, he knew that he trusted her. She would never do anything to hurt him. All he had to do was make up for the pain he had caused her so they could make a new start without the past tainting it.

First thing in the morning, they would have a long talk and straighten everything out. He would tell her that he cared for her and, more importantly, that he trusted her.

He shivered. He'd been standing here stark naked for too long. He went back to bed and slid under the covers, confident that by tomorrow night he would have his wife back in bed next to him. With a sigh, he settled back into his pillow. Within a minute, he was fast asleep.

Down the hall, Rebecca was wide-awake and staring at a crack in the ceiling. She'd been focused on that same crack for a while now and it hadn't changed. She'd cried herself out about an hour ago.

She was glad she'd made it to the guestroom before she'd broken down. She didn't want Jake to see her cry. He'd hurt her too much already. The really sad part was that he would probably have no idea why she was crying. Her heart was breaking, but the loss of her dreams hurt her even more.

Her own mother had left when she was five years old. She barely remembered her at all, except as a vague image of flowery perfume and pretty clothes. Rebecca's father hadn't been able to provide much in the way of extras. As a seasonal worker it had been all he could do to keep a roof over his family's head. Maybe that's why her mother had left. Maybe she wanted more than life had given her.

Rebecca sighed and rolled onto her side. All she knew was, as a child, she had needed her mother, and her mother hadn't been there. There was no way she would let that happen to Casey. No matter what happened, she was determined to remain a part of the child's life. That is, she amended, if Jake would let her.

She didn't know what else to do. She had loved Jake for years, but it was becoming painfully obvious to her that he might like her, but he didn't trust her or care for her or— heaven forbid—love her the way she wanted or needed him to. He didn't know her at all. If he did, there was no way he would ever have accused her of neglecting Casey. Her heart sank even further.

She shivered as she remembered the cold, accusing look in his eyes. How he had angrily blamed her for caring more about her business than about Casey. Well, she knew now what he really thought about her and her business. The only question that remained was what she going to do about the whole situation?

Over the last seven years, Jake had played a huge role in her life, even if he hadn't been aware of it. Her mind was filled with images of her and Jake, talking and laughing, spending time in each other's company. She'd come to depend on his unswerving friendship, but if she left she would lose it forever. They would politely speak when they passed each other in town, but that would be it. Their friendship would not survive the end of their marriage.

She could barely think about it. She hugged her pillow tighter wishing it were Jake. It was ironic that she was facing the biggest crisis of her life and couldn't talk to her best friend about it. That was another dilemma. Not only would she be losing the man that she loved, but she would be losing her best friend as well. She would be alone. Well, not totally alone, she reassured herself as she patted her belly.

That was another major problem. Jake wouldn't let her leave if he knew about the baby. He was an honorable man and would insist on staying married so he could support her and the baby. His sense of responsibility was huge. He had never hesitated for a minute to take Casey, and he'd been looking out for Rebecca since the night of her prom when he'd rescued her from her date.

But she couldn't live with the father of her child knowing that he didn't trust her to take good care of their child. She shivered. She needed to be more than a housekeeper. She needed to be loved and trusted by her husband.

"Stop it," she muttered aloud. "It's no good to work yourself up over what might be."

Jake. Even his name made her heart pound faster. She had no idea why he was acting this way. He had always been good to her, kind, and so very gentle. Since their marriage, they'd had a lot of ups and downs. Just when she thought they were making progress, he lashed out at her.

There were many birthdays and holidays she would have spent alone if it hadn't been for Jake. He had always turned up at her apartment with little presents and surprises. Like the exquisite flower he had carved for her. A man only did something like that for someone he cared about. That delicate carving, shaped from a simple, rough piece of wood, had always given her hope.

Then there were the apples during harvest time. He always brought her fresh, juicy apples so she could make pies. He had taken her to pick out her pumpkin on Halloween, waiting patiently as she looked at dozens before finding just the right one. There had been treks into the woods before Christmas to find the perfect tree for her little apartment. Thoughtful Christmas presents like a scarf or a pair of gloves meant a lot to her because she knew he picked them out himself. He had to care about her. He had to.

Somehow, since they had married, he had changed towards her. It was as if, now that she was his wife, he no longer trusted her. She was out of ideas on how to change things. She had been patient, understanding, and loving, but he still found her lacking.

Her biggest error, she decided, had been mistaking marital relations for intimacy. She thought they had been forging a deeper, caring relationship, while it seems as if he was just taking what was offered. She couldn't even blame him for that. He had offered her nothing, and she had asked for nothing.

Like the Jake of old, he was always gentle and considerate when they made love. She had even tricked herself into believing that he might be starting to love her a little. She had been wrong. Oh, he cared about her as a person, but not as a wife or as the mother of his children.

She didn't have any time to decide what she was going to do. She had to settle this in her mind right now. Between morning sickness and her changing shape, Jake would soon know she was pregnant. Not that she planned to keep him away from his child, but she could not risk him knowing about the child before she knew how he really felt about her, before she knew if their marriage had a chance.

She burrowed down deeper under the covers, trying to find some warmth. She was cold. It was a deep chill that came from the inside out and she wondered if she'd ever feel warm again. The look in Jake's eyes and his words had frozen her soul. She never wanted to see that look again. She didn't know if she'd survive it a second time. After yesterday, she wondered if he would even miss her if she left.

Her teeth began to chatter at the thought. She couldn't bear it if he asked her to leave. Maybe she should leave first. She honestly didn't know if he would realize how much he cared for her, or if he would consider himself well rid of her. It was a sad statement on her marriage that she couldn't say for sure what his reaction to her departure would be.

She rubbed a hand across her forehead. All this thinking had made her throbbing headache worse. She knew she wasn't ready to face Jake tomorrow morning. Things could not go on the way they were. Better that she leave now, after a couple months of marriage, than after two years, or twenty years.

If she stayed, she didn't know if she could live with herself or if she would always feel as if she settled for less than she deserved. She deserved to be loved. But she didn't know if he would ever love her, or if that was nothing more than a young girl's dream.

She could think no more. The sun would be rising in less than an hour and as much as her mind needed to think, her body wanted to sleep. The exhaustion of the day's events and her pregnancy demanded she rest.

Just before she finally drifted off into a fitful sleep, she grasped her pillow tighter, wishing again it were Jake. He would warm her up in no time, wrap her in his strong arms, and she would feel safe. Or maybe not. Maybe she would never feel safe in his arms again. Her last thought was that in the morning she would know what to do. In the morning, she would decide.

Chapter Fifteen

Rubbing the back of his neck, Jake tried to work out the knots of tension. Damn, but he hadn't meant to be gone all day. His good intentions had come to nothing. But with how things had been going lately, he shouldn't be surprised.

Planning to talk to Rebecca as soon as she got up, he'd been out of bed just as the sun was coming up over the horizon. After two cups of coffee, it became obvious that she was either still asleep or she wasn't coming down until he left. The thought that it was the latter annoyed him. He'd been ready to make amends and he'd had no one to apologize to. After a third cup and a lot of pacing, he decided that maybe it would be better to give her the day to cool off. He had grabbed his coat and left the house, spending the morning out in the orchards and the afternoon in town, running errands.

As he turned the truck up the driveway, he wondered if it hadn't been a mistake to stay away all day. Maybe he should have waited this morning until Rebecca had gotten out of bed. Maybe he should have come home for lunch. He sighed. So many maybes.

The house was dark and seemed unnaturally still as he pulled the truck to a stop near the back door. Rebecca was probably working in her sewing room, but a tingle of unease slid down his spine, urging him to hurry. He berated himself for being silly as he stepped down from the seat and closed the cab door. He would go in the house, and Rebecca and Casey would greet him in the kitchen, and they would all pitch in to make something for supper. After eating together, they would put Casey to bed, and then they would talk.

Still, he hurried up the back steps. The house was too quiet, as if all the life was gone from it. That last thought made the hair on the back of his neck stand on end.

Urgently now, he reached out and pushed the back door. It didn't budge. Did Rebecca think she could lock him out of his own home? The thought stopped him in his tracks. Finally common sense took hold. Maybe she had called Dani and gone shopping. Yeah, that had to be it. *Got to calm down*, he thought, as he unlocked the door and let himself into the kitchen.

He hung his coat on a peg just inside the door and headed for the refrigerator. Opening the door, he peered inside. He would make something for supper. That should help soften Rebecca up for their talk. He wondered if she'd like eggs and bacon for supper. His only other option was soup. He was good at preparing canned soup and crackers. He supposed he could grill a steak if he was really ambitious, but there wasn't time to thaw meat in time for supper.

He pulled out the eggs and bacon and placed them on the kitchen counter. As he reached down into the cupboard for a frying pan, he saw the white notepaper folded on the table with his name written neatly across it. It seemed Rebecca had even left him a note to let him know where they were gone. He opened it quickly, hoping she had given him some idea of when she would be home and that he had enough time to surprise her with supper.

He snatched up the note and started to read. He felt all the blood drain from his face and he grabbed the table for support as his legs started to give out on him. He eased himself into a kitchen chair to keep from falling into a heap on the floor. She wasn't coming home. Ever. She had left him. He read the note again, as if somehow the words might have changed since the first reading.

Dear Jake,

You can pick Casey up at my old apartment above Greer's. It has become painfully obvious to me that I am not the wife you want or need. I wish to remain part of Casey's life and, if you will let me, I will continue to baby-sit her every day for you. That is if you will trust me with her. If you do not, I will understand, but I hope you will still let me see Casey, as I love her very much.

You can have an uncontested divorce. All I ever wanted from you was your trust and, maybe in time, your love. But it is obvious that will never happen. I cannot make you happy. All I can do is set you free. Maybe in time you will find someone else to make you happy.

Love always,
Rebecca

Dear Lord, he had lost her. He sat there in the kitchen unable to fully comprehend what it meant. He broke out into a sweat. Not to have Rebecca in his life was unthinkable. She had been a part of his life for years now. The only bright spot in his bleak and lonely existence.

He measured his life by the times they spent together, by the holidays and special times they shared. She had brought this old house to life and made it a home for the first time in his memory. She had added light and warmth to his life and now it was gone.

How long he sat there, he didn't know. But by the time he regained some of his senses, the kitchen was in total darkness. His breathing was harsh, as if he'd run for miles, and his chest hurt. He lifted his hand to try and ease the ache and was surprised to find the note crumpled in his left fist. Forcing his fingers to release their grip on the paper, he carefully smoothed it out and laid it on the table as he rose unsteadily to his feet.

Still in darkness, he made his way to the stairs. Trudging upstairs to their room, he reluctantly opened the closet door. All her clothes were gone. He ran his fingers over the empty hangers. They swung back and forth, mocking him with the memory of their former fullness. He missed them. He had liked the intimacy of her clothes hanging next to his. He checked the bathroom door. Her nightgown and robe were missing from the brass hook where she always hung them. Her hairbrush and all the little bottles of creams and things that she'd had lined up on the counter were no longer there.

Jake ran his hand over the bare counter. The tile felt cold under his hand. He liked sharing the bathroom with Rebecca. Having her pretty bottles next to his shaving gear had given him a sense of belonging. He glanced in the mirror and saw his own pale reflection staring back at him. His eyes were red and haunted. His mouth was tight. It was a grim sight.

His legs carried him back into the bedroom and he sank down onto the edge of the bed. The house seemed colder with her gone. Physically, he knew that the temperature in the house was the same as always, but the warmth and the life were gone. He buried his face in his hands, trying to make sense of it all. Her scent—vanilla, sunshine and woman—wafted up from the unmade bed. It was the same smell that had kept him awake last night. Rebecca.

His jaw hardened as he ground his teeth together. They were a family and they would remain a family. That thought propelled him to his feet and down the stairs. Slamming the back door behind him, he jumped in the truck and headed for town.

He would apologize and she would come home. It was as simple as that. He'd been wrong to put off talking to her this morning. He could see that now. She had a right to be angry with him, but she shouldn't have run away. His hands clenched the steering wheel so tight all his knuckles were white. He would not even consider the possibility that she had left him for good.

This was just her way of letting him know that she was angry with him. He would explain everything to her, and she and Casey would come home with him. He forced himself to ease his grip on the wheel and took a deep breath to calm himself.

And what about Casey? She must sense that something was wrong. She was a sensitive child and this certainly couldn't be good for her either. She needed to know that she was secure, that they were a family.

Halting the truck in front of Greer's Grocery, he was onto the asphalt and up the stairs before the vehicle had rocked to a full stop.

Pounding on the door he called out her name. "Rebecca. Open the door, Rebecca." The door jerked open as he pulled back his hand to hit it again.

Rebecca, her eyes wide in her pale face, stared at Jake and swallowed hard. He looked angry. Very angry. Like a wild bull out of control, his breathing was hard and his fists were clenched. She knew he might not trust her with Casey, but she hadn't expected him to come banging on her door to drag the child away so quickly. Just looking at him was difficult. She swallowed her tears and forced herself to speak calmly.

"Come in, Jake. I'll have Casey ready to go in a minute." She turned and walked away from the door. He could either come in or wait outside. At this point, she didn't care which.

Pushing his way into the kitchen, Jake didn't even bother to close the door behind him. He obviously didn't expect to be here long. "Fine, we can talk when we get home."

She spun back around, not believing what he'd said. "What do you mean 'we'?"

"We, as in all of us." He glared at her as if daring her to disagree with him.

"Why should I go back with you?"

Her soft-spoken question seemed to strike him like a fist to his gut. "Why? Why?"

She swallowed hard. In spite of his anger, this question was too important for her not to ask. "Yes, why?"

"Because you're my wife and you belong with me and Casey." He nodded for emphasis.

"You didn't seem to want me there yesterday and I was your wife then too." Rebecca still shuddered when she recalled the look Jake had given her when he'd accused her of neglecting Casey.

Jake took a deep breath, obviously trying to calm himself. "Look, I know I was out of line yesterday. I waited to talk to you this morning, but you didn't come down."

"I didn't get to sleep until early morning and I overslept." She tilted her chin up, daring him to criticize her for her seeming laziness.

He nodded in understanding. "I didn't get much sleep myself last night. I missed you."

The last was said in a deep husky voice that she felt to the tips of her toes. She wanted to fling herself in his arms, but instead she forced herself to stand her ground. "What did you want to talk about?"

Jake started to reach for her, sighed and stuffed his hands in his jacket pockets instead. "I wanted to apologize for what I said yesterday. I never really meant it." He watched her as she nodded with a quiet acceptance. "So now we can go home."

It took him a moment to comprehend that she was shaking her head at him and that this time she wasn't saying yes. "What do you mean, no?" he demanded. "I said I was sorry. What more do you want?"

Rebecca shook her head sadly. "I know you're sorry *now* for what you said, but I'm not altogether sure you didn't mean part of it."

Jake started to speak, but she forestalled him. "It's true, Jake. Since we got married you've changed. I feel like I'm constantly being measured against some imaginary scale and I always come up short."

"That's not true." Even as he spoke those words, Rebecca somehow knew that he had been measuring her against the other women in his life who had let him down.

"Yes, it is true, Jake. I don't like feeling like I have to earn your trust and your affection and your..." She couldn't bring herself to say love, because she knew he didn't love her. "Respect," she finished quickly.

Straightening her shoulders, she stood tall as her pride filled her. "You've treated this as a business deal from the first and I went along with you, thinking we could build something good out of it." She slumped just a little. "But, I was wrong. When all the trust and caring is on one side, there's no hope."

Jake pulled his hands from his pockets and gently grasped her by the shoulders. "I do care. You know that."

"I thought you did. But that isn't enough if you don't trust me." She turned away from him and looked out the small kitchen window. It was strange to see the cars and the people in the parking lot below. People going about the business of grocery shopping and chatting with friends and neighbors. How normal it all seemed when her whole life was falling apart.

Rebecca felt as if her life was slipping away from her. As if he couldn't help himself, he stood behind her and wrapped his arms around her, trying to bind her to him physically. Leaning down, he whispered in her ear.

"Come home, sweetheart." He played his trump card. "I know you love Casey," he paused, "and me. Come home where you belong." He hugged her tight. She knew he felt certain of her answer. Of course she would come home now. Everything was worked out as far as he was concerned.

"I can't." Her voice broke on a sob.

"Of course you can," he soothed, rubbing his hands up and down her arms. "Why not?" he demanded calmly when she shook her head again. Rebecca was certain Jake felt he could smooth over all her worries and they would soon be on their way home. He kissed her neck gently.

"It won't work, Jake. I can't come back until you can give me the reason I need."

Jake straightened and released her. "I've already given you two good reasons."

"It's not enough. I need more than that from you."

His voice was gruff, his exasperation evident as he spoke. "What game are you playing? Tell me what you want me to say and we can go home."

She knew he didn't understand what she wanted and it wasn't something she could tell him. Either he loved and trusted her or he didn't.

"Tell me what to say."

"I can't." She wrapped her arms tightly around herself. "If you don't know I can't tell you."

She could tell Jake didn't know what to do. Anger, disappointment and even a tinge of what seemed to be fear, flashed across his face. He was finally coming to grips with the reality that she wasn't coming home with him.

Swallowing hard, he spoke. "So what do we do from here?"

"I don't know. I only know I can't live the way I have been living." She faltered and her voice broke. "I just don't know."

"Uncle Jake! Uncle Jake!"

The sound of Casey's voice snapped Jake's gaze towards the bedroom door. He reached down and caught the child up in his arms as she hurtled herself towards him, hugging her tight to him.

Rebecca struggled to regain her composure. Watching the two of them together almost broke her heart. She knew Jake loved Casey. It was obvious in the way he held her and spoke to her. She wished he could love her that way as well.

"Hi, honey. Where were you?" He kissed the top of her curly head.

"I fell asleep," she answered shyly.

Her answer made him smile. "And what have you and Aunt Rebecca been doing today?"

While Casey launched into a full report of the day, he listened to her but his eyes never left Rebecca.

"It sounds like you had a good day," he commented when Casey finished up. He hugged her again and then placed her gently on the floor. "I've got to go out for a while. You stay here with Aunt Rebecca for now and I'll be back for you later." Jake glanced at her. "Is that okay with you?"

Startled by the quick change in conversation and the flatness of his voice, she just nodded. She watched as he bent and gave Casey a quick kiss and then he was gone. His footsteps on the stairs sounded as hollow as her heart felt.

Unless he could tell her and show her he loved her, she couldn't go back. Not now when there was so much more at stake. Her hand drifted to her stomach. She would never keep him from his child, but neither would she trap him into staying married just because she was pregnant. She couldn't survive a loveless marriage, for the children would suffer most of all in such an arrangement. It would be cold comfort without the warmth, a household instead of a home.

Right now she had another child to worry about. "How about we go downstairs to the grocery store and pick out something for supper?" Casey quickly nodded and ran to get her sneakers, leaving Rebecca alone in the kitchen, staring out the window, and wondering where they all went from here.

Chapter Sixteen

Jake glanced up at the window as he drove away. Rebecca was watching him from the window. He wanted to go back up there and throw her over his shoulder and drag her home. He would too, except he knew she would just leave him again.

He banged his fist on the steering wheel in utter frustration. He honestly didn't know what to do. The look of pain on her face when he'd asked her what he could say to make her come home had almost brought him too his knees.

Her pain had flowed through him and he hadn't been able to stay any longer. He rolled his shoulders, trying to release some of the tension from his body. It was a useless gesture. The only thing that would help him would be for Rebecca to come home. But more than that, he wanted to remove the pain from her beautiful blue eyes and make her smile again. Her happiness was everything to him.

He loved her.

It had been right in front of him for years, but he'd been too blind to see. Too busy trying to protect his own heart, he'd never realized that it was already too late. His heart belonged to Rebecca.

How could he not have known? He had been lying to himself for the past seven years. Of course, he loved her.

How could he not, when she had brought such joy and happiness into his life? And now it was gone.

He swallowed hard. Not quite gone, yet.

With that thought came resolve. He stared down the long dark road ahead of him. No, damn it, he could not lose her. He wouldn't lose her.

There had to be a way to win her back. All he had to do was think of it. He already had two powerful things on his side. One was that Rebecca loved him. He knew that now. In his heart he'd always known that was why she had married him. The other was that Rebecca loved Casey as well. In a short time, Rebecca had begun to think of herself as Casey's mother.

He had to find a way to make up for all the pain he had caused her in their short marriage. From the very beginning, he had protected himself from becoming too close. Even their wedding had been rushed, almost business-like. Their wedding night had been days later.

Looking back, he was ashamed at how he had handled the whole affair. In trying to protect himself, he had not only hurt Rebecca, but himself as well. They were meant to be together. Too bad he hurt them both before he had been able to figure that out.

He needed time to think and decide what to do. Time to figure out the words she needed to hear. First of all, he had to find some way to let her know that he trusted her. He would build on that foundation.

He brought the truck to a halt in back of the house, which looked bleak and forlorn. There were no lights shining from the windows or warm welcome waiting for him. Rebecca wouldn't be there to give him a hug or a smile as she asked about his day. He'd come to depend on her unconditional love, grown addicted to her sweet kisses. He was reluctant to go in, but he knew there was no other choice. Slowly, he walked up the back steps and let himself into the kitchen.

He took his time, hanging up his coat and putting on a pot of coffee. His stomach growled, so he wandered to the refrigerator. The carton of eggs and the package of bacon were still lying on the counter where he'd left them. Picking up the bacon, he shrugged. He'd planned to cook this for supper earlier; he might as well eat it himself.

The idea came to him while he was flipping his eggs over easy. He pondered it while he chewed on the bacon and toast. He turned it over in his mind as he sipped his coffee. The more he thought about it the more he liked it.

Turning toward the counter, he picked up the phone and dialed before he gave himself time to think. He had her old number dialed before he realized it was no longer in service. Reaching behind him he pulled open a kitchen drawer and grabbed the phone book. He looked up Greer's Grocery and Gas Bar and dialed the number.

Jake hated to have to leave a message for Rebecca. It took more than a little persuasion on his part, but he finally got a reluctant Mr. Greer to agree to pass on the message. It would have been easier to go into town and see her again, but he knew he wasn't ready yet. He didn't think he could see her and not throw her over his shoulder and bring her home with him. That would accomplish nothing. Well, he amended, it might help the short term, but he was in this for the long haul.

Pouring another cup of coffee, he paced the floor with his cup in his hand while he mentally willed the phone to ring. He glanced at his watch every few minutes. Fifteen minutes later, the phone finally rang. His hand shook as he lifted the receiver.

"Rebecca?"

"Yes, it's me." Her voice was a trembling whisper on the other end of the line.

When she said no more, he knew it was up to him to break the silence. "Rebecca, I want you to do a favor for me."

Rebecca was momentarily stunned into silence. He knew, of all the things he could have said, this was not what she had expected. When she recovered her senses enough to speak, she answered without hesitation. "If I can," she answered cautiously. "What do you want?"

He couldn't believe she had agreed so easily, but he realized he shouldn't have been surprised. Rebecca had always been a generous and giving woman where he was concerned. He set his coffee mug on the counter and ran his free hand through his already tousled hair. "I need a few days to myself. Can you keep Casey with you? I'll bring out some clothes and stuff in the morning." He held his breath as he waited for her reply.

"Of course I'll keep her for you. That is, if you trust me enough." she added.

"I've always trusted you, sweetheart. It was never a matter of trust," Jake answered softly.

"I don't understand, Jake."

"I know you don't, honey, but you will. Kiss Casey for me and tell her I'll see her in the morning, okay? Sleep tight, Rebecca, and think about me." Jake hung up the phone before he broke down and ordered her to come home to him. He had to do this right.

Rebecca felt tears flow down her face as his endearment pierced her heart. Their conversation ended quickly and she was left listening to the dial tone on the other end. He had hung up. What did he mean, think of him? Of course, she was thinking of him. It was all she was doing.

Pulling herself together, she went to the front of the store where Casey was playing under the watchful eye of Mr. Greer. As a grandfather five times over, he was more than up to the task. The concern on his face when he had brought the message that Jake wanted her to call him had almost made her start crying all over again. It was all she could do to murmur her thanks to him and hustle Casey back upstairs. She was grateful he hadn't questioned her, but then, he hadn't asked her any questions when she'd asked for her old apartment back. Fortunately for her, not many people were looking to rent apartments in Jamesville, especially not one over a busy grocery store and gas station. Mr. Greer had just handed her the keys and told her to be sure and get some groceries before the store closed for the night. He had always been kind to her.

She bit her lip to keep from crying. She didn't even know if Jake missed her. He'd given her no indication at all. She wondered why he wanted this time to himself. Perhaps, he was going to have divorce papers drawn up quickly. She didn't know, and she couldn't think about it right now. Her silence was causing Casey to look at her with worry in her eyes.

"You and I will stay here for a few days, okay? Uncle Jake will be out to see you in the morning and he'll bring some more of your clothes and toys with him." She tried her best to smile as she spoke.

"Will Uncle Jake stay with us too?" Casey asked.

"No, Casey. It's just you and me for a few days. Uncle Jake has some business to tend to." They entered the apartment and she locked the door behind her. "It'll be fun. Just us girls."

Rebecca was thankful that Casey easily accepted that explanation and sat on the floor to play with her little wooden rabbit. Watching her, Rebecca wished she could be comforted as easily.

The rest of the evening passed in a blur. It had been all she could do to keep up a cheerful front. Rebecca felt as if her face was permanently pulled more into a grimace than a smile. She'd had a hard time settling Casey in for the night and she knew that the little girl had sensed something was wrong. That and the nap she'd had earlier had kept Casey awake much later than her regular bedtime.

Finally, the little girl was asleep, tucked into a cot that Mr. Greer had brought up earlier. He kept it in the back office for when his own grandchildren came to visit and hadn't hesitated to let her borrow it. Assured that the child was sleeping soundly, Rebecca crept out of the bedroom, leaving the door open in case Casey called out.

Wandering into the living room, she looked out the window. It was ironic that she had stood in this same spot several months before, trying to decide if she should marry Jake. She had taken the gamble, but had lost.

She scrubbed her hands up and down her arms in a vain attempt to get warm. She had been cold all day and she knew no amount of heat would warm her again. She had lost the warmth of her new home and of Jake's caring, and she felt frozen all the way to her soul.

The only good she could see was that Jake seemed to trust her with Casey. If he didn't, he would have come and taken her. Instead, he had asked if the child could stay for a few days.

She freely admitted that she didn't understand Jake. She missed him and longed to feel his arms envelop her and hold her tight. When he'd wrapped them around her this evening, it had taken all her willpower not to beg him to take her home with him.

Loving him made it hard to resist him, but she had no other choice. A marriage built on a business arrangement was no marriage at all. She knew Jake's parents hadn't had a good marriage and neither had her own parents. It was the one thing she had vowed to avoid in her own life. Now everything was a mess. She was repeating their mistakes.

Looking up into the night sky, she watched the stars, hoping to find some answers. When the chill became too much and she started shivering, Rebecca finally gave up and crawled into bed.

She gazed at the cot next to the bed where Casey was snuggled under her blankets. Tightening the covers around herself, she tried not to make any noise as she attempted to warm herself.

Even her small bed seemed large without Jake beside her. Stacking pillows behind her, she tried to get comfortable. She lay on her side and placed her hands gently on her stomach. She had a doctor's appointment in two days time. She'd made it first thing this morning as she had forgotten to make it the morning Casey had run away.

Was that just yesterday? It seemed like a lifetime ago. Her life had changed so much in just a couple of days.

So much hope was gone. She'd have to tell Jake about the baby eventually, but right now she wanted to put it off as long as possible. She drifted off into a light sleep as she worried about the morning's confrontation with Jake.

Jake cleaned up from supper and went upstairs to bed. He showered and then crawled into bed to think. Propping his hands behind his head, he stared at the ceiling. He had an idea of what he wanted to do, but it was somewhere after two when he hit on the perfect solution. A huge grin covered his face. He was brilliant. Absolutely brilliant.

It would work. It had to work because he couldn't live without Rebecca. His resolve hardened. He wouldn't live without her. He would make this work.

Reaching into the drawer next to the bed table, he pulled out a pad of paper and a pen. He spent the next hour making a list. He had a lot to do and not much time in which to accomplish it. But he did know several people who would help him.

With plans still rolling around in his head, he fell asleep. The pen and paper slipped out of his hands and hit the floor when he turned over in bed.

Chapter Seventeen

Rebecca stood at the kitchen counter, buttering a slice of toast, as she waited for the kettle to boil. She might as well have stayed up all night, she thought crossly, for all the sleep she'd gotten. Over and over, she'd thought about what she'd done. She had been right to leave Jake. In her heart she knew she had done everything to make their marriage work. The next move, if there was one, had to come from Jake. She just wasn't sure if he thought it was worth the effort.

The whistle of the boiling kettle pulled her back to the present. She looked at the toast and pushed the plate away. With her head pounding and her stomach tied up in knots, there was no way she would even attempt to eat anything yet. Not until Jake had come and gone. She didn't want to lose her breakfast while he was here, so she wasn't taking any chances. Her morning sickness was too unpredictable.

Pouring hot water into the "Happy Birthday" mug Jake had given her last year, she absently stirred the tea bag around. Arrangements would have to be made for the return of her sewing equipment. As much as she dreaded to ask, it would be easier for everyone if Jake boxed it all up and delivered it to her.

She hated to ask anyone else for help. Her marriage problems were her own, but she knew it was only a matter of days before half the town knew she and Jake were separated. Still, she'd take whatever reprieve she could get. Part of her was still wishing for a miracle, hoping that this separation was temporary.

If she was truthful with herself, she was hoping Jake would insist she come home with him because he couldn't live without her. She sighed. It was a long shot, but it was all she had at the moment.

A knock on the door startled her, causing her to slosh hot tea over the counter and onto her hand.

"Ouch!"

Thrusting her burnt hand under the kitchen tap, she turned the cold water on. The relief was instantaneous.

The knock came again, more insistent this time. "Just a second," she called as the door swung open and Jake walked in.

"What took you so long?" Jake saw the spilled tea and her hand under the running water and bolted across the kitchen. He dropped the plastic bag he was carrying and reached for her hand. "Let me see."

Reluctantly, she gave him her injured hand. "It's all right. I was just startled when you knocked. It's hardly even red."

Jake paid no attention her, but continued to examine the damaged skin of her hand. It was small next to his, yet she placed it there trustingly. He raised her hand to his lips and gently kissed the small red spot. "I'm sorry you hurt yourself."

Rebecca was almost dizzy with emotion. Their marriage was on the verge of breaking up and he was worried about a minor burn on her hand. She drew her hand back quickly. "I'm fine."

She turned and grabbed a dishcloth and wiped up the spilled tea from the counter. "I'm having tea, but I can put on a pot of coffee."

Jake retrieved the plastic grocery bag he'd dropped on the floor. "No thanks, I can't stay."

"Oh." She didn't know what else to say. She wanted to ask him where he was going and why he wasn't staying, but she didn't think she had that right anymore. She bit her lip to keep from blurting out the questions.

"Casey's clothes and some toys are in here." He laid the bag on the table. "There's enough for two days. That should be plenty of time."

Now she was totally bewildered. "Plenty of time for what?"

"You'll see." He quickly changed the subject. "Casey's not up yet?"

"No, not yet." Rebecca dropped the cloth in the sink and clasped her hands in front of her to keep from wringing them together. Jake had her totally confused.

"I'll drop by and see her after supper. If that's okay with you?" he added.

"That's fine." She paused. "Jake, about my sewing equipment..."

"There's no hurry for it, is there?" He shoved his hands in his pockets and looked everywhere but at her.

"I really need it. If you don't have time, I can get someone else to move it for me." Being busy would give her less time to think, especially in the evenings after Casey was asleep.

Jake's jaw tightened and he took a deep breath before he spoke, his voice low and even. "I can drop it off when I pick Casey up tomorrow night. Is that soon enough?"

"That's fine, if you're sure it's no trouble?" she added. If his jaw got any tighter, it might crack. Jake was angry, but she wasn't quite sure why. Was it a bother for him to bring her things out to her? She rubbed her temples. It was too early in the morning to try and figure him out. He was giving her a headache.

"Listen, I've got to go. I've got a lot to do today. Give Casey a kiss for me and tell her I'll see her later." Reaching out, he took her by the shoulders and gave her a kiss. Not a quick peck, but the long, hot kind she'd been missing. When he drew away, he gave a satisfied grunt, seeming pleased by the bemused look she knew was on her face. He left quickly before she could ask any questions. Her curiosity would obviously have to wait.

She touched her lips in wonder. He had kissed her as if he missed her. She tried not to read too much into it. After all, it was just a kiss. But what a kiss, she sighed. Her lips still tingled. Shaking herself mentally, she went to check on Casey. Today would be a good day to go to the park. Anything but sitting around here all day and wondering and worrying about what Jake was going to do. She couldn't figure out what was going on inside Jake's head. Maybe the fresh air would help her headache.

Jake drove into town and parked his truck in front of Jessie's Diner. He'd had enough of his own cooking last night. And besides that, he figured if he needed any help, Jessie was one person who might help him.

Jessie smiled at him as he stepped into the warmth of the diner. "Find a seat and I'll bring you some coffee," she said as she breezed by him carrying a tray full of toast, eggs, pancakes and hash browns. Just his luck that the place was busy this morning. He probably wouldn't get much of a chance to talk with her until the crowd thinned after the breakfast rush.

He saw a booth by the window become empty as two local businessmen stood to leave. He ambled towards the table, nodding at people he knew as he went. He slid into the empty seat as Jessie bustled up behind him. In ten seconds flat, she had the table cleared and a fresh cup of coffee sitting in front of him.

"What will you have this morning? The special is blueberry pancakes, bacon and juice."

Jake smiled at the thought and rubbed his empty stomach. Jessie's blueberry pancakes were legendary. "The special with orange juice sounds good to me."

She nodded as she wrote down the order and shoved the pad into her apron pocket. "How are Rebecca and Casey this morning? They were in the other day, but I didn't get a chance to talk with them." She tucked the pen behind her right ear. "I've been real busy lately and it's harder to keep up with things with Shannon gone."

"They're doing good." He paused for a second and focused on straightening the napkin on the table in front of him. "Jessie, can I talk to you about something? I'll wait until the crowd clears out."

"Sure you can." Jessie looked intrigued, but she was also busy, "I'll get your breakfast and I should be able to get a break in about an hour or so."

"That's fine." He let go of the napkin and met her warm smile. "And thanks, Jessie." Jessie nodded and hustled away to refill the coffee cups of the couple at the next table.

Jake took out the list he'd started last night and unfolded it. Smoothing it out, he laid it on the table and studied it. He didn't look up when Jessie brought his breakfast, other than to say thanks. He wished he knew if he was doing this right. He really needed another opinion, but he decided he might as well enjoy his breakfast while he waited for Jessie.

The pancakes tasted like a piece of heaven—light, fluffy and bursting with blueberries. He was finishing the last bite when a shadow fell across his table.

Burke Black was standing there with a huge smile on his usually somber face. "Why don't you sit down and tell me the good news?" Jake found himself smiling for no reason as he motioned to the seat across from him.

"How did you know?" Burke asked as he slid into the seat across from Jake. He folded his big hands on the table in front of him as he glanced around for Jessie.

"Know what?"

"The good news," Burke replied.

Jake laughed. "I don't know anything except that the look on your face tells me something good happened."

"Dani had the baby, a boy. We're going to call him Shane Patrick."

Jake stuck out his hand to Burke. "Congratulations. When did it happen?"

Burke took the hand extended to him. "Early yesterday morning. I got home from your place just in time to take Dani to the hospital." He laughed. "Dani did great. I just wasn't sure I'd make it."

Jake found that he envied Burke. He pictured Rebecca holding their child in her arms. That was what he wanted, the same kind of family life that Burke had found with Dani. "You and Dani have a great marriage, don't you?" he asked cautiously.

"Yeah, we do. It didn't start out that way, though." Burke looked thoughtful for a second, obviously remembering some private memories. "Why do you ask?"

Jake didn't answer right away as Jessie came up to their table with a cup for Burke and a pot of fresh coffee to refill Jake's cup as well.

"Any breakfast this morning, Burke? I imagine you're on your way to the hospital to see Dani and Baby Shane after you leave here. You tell them I said hello and I'll be out to see the baby as soon as I can." Jessie filled both cups as she spoke.

"Thanks, Jessie. I know Dani would like that. I guess I'll have whatever the special is." When Jessie left, Burke looked back at Jake, waiting for his reply.

Jake took a deep breath. It wasn't easy for him to talk to anyone but Rebecca about his problems, and she couldn't help him with this. "I don't understand women."

Burke started to laugh, his whole body shaking with mirth. "My friend, I may be married, but I still don't understand women."

Jake chuckled. "Yeah, but your wife is happy." He sobered immediately. "Mine's left me."

"I'm sorry." Burke stared at his coffee, obviously not knowing what else to say.

"It's my own fault and it's only temporary." He glared at the other man as if daring him to disagree. "I'm going to fix it."

"So, what are you going to do?" Burke blew on his coffee and took a sip.

"I've got a plan, but I need some help." His hand automatically covered the list on the table.

Burke responded instantly. "Is there anything I can do to help?"

"Look at this list for me and see if I've left anything out." He pushed the slip of paper across the table.

Burke picked up the list and slowly read it from top to bottom. He looked confused as he studied it. "I'm not sure I understand what you're trying to do here."

Jake sighed. "We didn't do it right the first time and that's part of the problem. I need to show her how much she means to me."

"Have you told her how you feel?"

"It wouldn't be enough. I've got to show her. I've got to make her see." Jake was sure this was the right way to go about things.

Burke looked doubtful. "I still think you should just tell the woman you're in love with her. But if this is what you're going to do, you'll need a dress."

"How am I gonna pick out a dress?"

The sound of feminine laughter made Jake lift his head. "I think you'll want something long, to cover your hairy legs." Jessie winked at Burke as she laid his plate of pancakes in front of him.

"It's not for me, it's for Rebecca." He scowled at Jessie and then reluctantly smiled when he saw the twinkle in her eyes.

"I kind of figured that. Is that what you wanted to ask me earlier? You want me to help you pick out a dress for Rebecca?"

Jake looked up at Jessie. "That's not quite what I wanted to talk to you about, but I would be forever in your debt if you would." He laughed. "Somehow, I can't see myself going into Lucy's Boutique and picking out a dress. But," he added seriously, "I'd do it if I had to."

"What's the dress for?"

Burke interrupted the two of them. "Jessie, I think you'd better grab a cup of coffee and sit down. This could take a while."

Bemused but curious, she did just that. When she understood Jake's plan, she grabbed a pen and started to make another list. Within half an hour it was all planned, at least on paper.

"So, I'll take care of these things," she waved her list in the air.

"You're sure it's not too much trouble?" He was relieved to have Jessie take over some of the planning. He had enough on his own list to keep him busy for the next two days.

"Of course it's no trouble. You take care of the things on your list and I'll take care of the things on mine." Jessie got up from the booth. "Now, I've got work to do and phone calls to make." She bent over and kissed Jake's cheek. "I'll see you tomorrow. Don't you worry about a thing."

He felt the color rise in his cheek as Jessie kissed him. He looked across the table at Burke, who just sat there grinning at him. Jake suddenly realized that he had a good friend in the man who sat across from him. "Thanks for listening."

"You're welcome, Jake. When this is all over and Dani's been home for a while, you'll have to bring your family over for supper." Burke finished his coffee, pushed his plate away, and got up from the table. "I'm off to the hospital to visit my family. Call if you need anything else."

He started to pull out his wallet, but Jake stopped him. "It's on me. And thanks again for everything." He offered his hand to Burke to seal the deal. "You'll be here tomorrow afternoon?" Jake asked.

"After all the trouble you're going to I wouldn't miss it for the world, and if Doctor Parker gives her okay, I know Dani will be here too." With that, Burke strode out of the diner waving at Jessie as he left.

Jake sat there for a moment, feeling hopeful for the first time in days. This would work. It had to, because the alternative was unacceptable. He drank down the last of his coffee and strode purposefully to the counter to pay for breakfast. He had work to do.

Chapter Eighteen

Rebecca turned as the door swished shut behind her. Hoisting her purse higher on her shoulder, she faced the front of the elevator. Leaning forward, she pressed the button for the hospital maternity ward. Eyes forward, she ignored the other two people who rode with her.

Her mind was a constant turmoil. Fiddling with her purse strap, she tried to put Jake out of her mind, but it was impossible. He had looked incredibly handsome earlier tonight when he'd come to visit with Casey. She could hardly bear to be in the same room with him. It hurt too much. When he had casually mentioned that Dani had had her baby, she'd jumped at the chance to go visit her friend. Not only did she want to see Dani, but it also got her away from Jake and those feelings of desire he stirred in her.

The door swished open and she stepped out into the hallway. She wrinkled her nose as the smell of antiseptic hit her. Hospitals always smelled the same no matter what floor you were on. A quick stop at the nurses' desk gave her the room number, and a few short steps later she was standing outside the closed door. As she raised her hand to knock, it occurred to her that in a little over six months from now she would be in Dani's position. It was a sobering proposition, especially knowing she would be giving birth alone with no husband to share it with her.

She knocked on the door and waited until Dani called out for her to come in. Plastering a smile on her face, she pushed the door open and poked her head in. "How's the new mother?"

Dani smiled when she saw Rebecca at the door. "I'm absolutely wonderful."

"You certainly are," Burke seconded from the chair next to the bed.

Dani laughed and waved Rebecca into the room. "Come and see Shane Patrick." She motioned to the bundle in Burke's arms. "That is if Dad there will let you see him."

Rebecca swallowed hard as she caught the look they sent to one another. It was filled with such love that it almost hurt to watch them. She slowly walked over to where Burke sat and looked down at the newborn infant held so carefully in his arms.

"Oh, he's beautiful." She knew that was the standard line all people used when discussing new babies, but she couldn't help herself. In this case it was true. The baby's hair was coal black; his eyes dark blue. "He looks just like you, Burke."

"Yeah, he's a handsome little guy all right." The fierce pride Burke felt was evident on his face, as he held the child secure in his arms. The love glowed in his eyes as he looked at his son.

Dani gazed indulgently at her husband. "You're so modest." She turned to Rebecca. "So what's new with you?"

Rebecca couldn't stop staring at the baby. She was picturing herself holding her own child in her arms, but unlike Dani and Burke, she would have no loving husband to share the experience with. Oh, Jake would love the child and be concerned about her, but it wasn't the same. Not the same at all.

Pulling her gaze away, she answered Dani. "It's still hard to get used to the fact that Casey is talking, but she seems to be recovered from her ordeal." She didn't want to talk about her problems, at least not in front of Burke.

Not wishing to pursue that line of questioning, she pulled her purse off her shoulder and dug through it. A quick search produced a small package, which she handed to Dani. "This is a little something for you."

Reaching out, her friend took the gaily-wrapped package and began to open it. "Thank you, but you didn't need to buy anything." She opened the small box, pushing the tissue paper out of the way. "It's beautiful, Rebecca." Carefully, she took the small silver frame out of the box. The frame had a teddy bear etched in one corner and building blocks in another.

Dani held it up for her husband to see. "Look, it's for Shane's picture."

Burke looked at the frame and then smiled at Rebecca. "It's beautiful and thoughtful. Thank you." He stared at her for a long moment, until she began to squirm uncomfortably under his intense scrutiny. "Are you all right? You look a little pale."

Before she could answer him, the door opened and a nurse poked her head through the opening. "It's time to take the baby back to the nursery."

Burke jumped at the opportunity to leave the women alone to talk. "I'll take Shane back down and then run down to the cafeteria for a cup of coffee while you've got company."

Dani shot her husband a knowing look that said "thank you" as he bent and kissed her on the forehead. He held the baby low enough to allow her to kiss Shane. "I'll see you in a few hours, little one."

"I'll be back in a while, but if you're gone before I get back, thanks again for the present and for coming to visit." Burke left, holding his son in his arms, talking to him as he went.

Rebecca was strangely ill at ease after Burke left the room. She didn't want Dani to know that anything was wrong, so she tried to steer the conversation away from herself and ended up chattering instead. "So how are you feeling? Was the labor long? How soon are you going home?"

"Fine, not too long, and hopefully tomorrow. Now will you please tell me what's wrong and don't say 'nothing'." Her friend settled the covers more securely over herself and then gave Rebecca a pointed look.

Rebecca didn't know where to begin, so she blurted it out. "I've left Jake."

"You've what?" Dani sat up straight in the bed, her eyes huge. "But you love Jake," she paused. "Don't you?"

Rebecca rubbed her hands up and down her arms trying to warm herself. No matter what she did, she was cold. She looked up at her friend, certain that all the painful emotions swamping her were mirrored in her eyes. "Of course I love him. I have for years."

"Then why did you leave him? What happened?"

Rebecca could tell that her friend was totally confused. "It's a long story."

Dani motioned to the hospital bed and scooted to one side to make room for her. "I'm not going anywhere."

Rebecca settled herself on the edge of the bed and it all came pouring out of her. The reason Jake had proposed, the quick wedding, the way he blamed her for Casey's running away, everything. Well, not quite everything. She didn't tell Dani about her wedding night or about the baby. She couldn't tell anyone about the baby until she worked up the nerve to tell Jake. He deserved to be the first to know. She finally ended the story with her decision to leave her husband.

"And the worst thing is, I don't even know what he thinks or what he's going to do next." She was out of breath when she finished. Her hands were shaking slightly and she knew she was pale.

Dani listened with amazement to her story. "I had no idea." She shook her head and mulled over what Rebecca had told her. "Well, whatever the reason, he did ask you to marry him. That means he's got to have some feelings for you."

Rebecca nodded. "I guess."

"And," she continued. "He did apologize for blaming you for Casey's disappearance."

Again, Rebecca slowly nodded.

"So, maybe he wants to have another chance to work things out." Dani took Rebecca's hand and gave it a squeeze.

"Do you think so?" Rebecca asked hopefully, wanting to believe her friend with all her heart. "I'm not so sure he cares one way or another."

"Maybe he doesn't know how to ask you to come back, or maybe he won't ask you outright. It could be that his pride will keep him from asking," she added as Rebecca's face fell.

"I honestly don't know what to think at this point. The fact that he left Casey with me gave me some hope, but he hasn't said anything about me going back with them when he finally comes to take her home." She rubbed her forehead. "All I've gotten out of this so far is a headache."

"Give it some time and see what happens." Dani gave her a helpless little shrug. "I know it's not great advice, but if you truly love him, you may have to fight for your marriage. That may mean going back with him and working on your problems no matter how long it takes."

Rebecca knew Dani was right, but what her friend didn't know was that she was short on time. If she'd only had herself to consider, she would have stayed until she was sure there was absolutely no hope. But now she had a child to think about and she didn't know if a marriage of convenience was the place to raise her child.

It wasn't fair to any of them and it especially wasn't fair to Casey. The little girl needed a loving home, not a home where her aunt and uncle were at odds. "There is something else to consider..."

The door opened and Shamus walked in carrying a bouquet of flowers before Rebecca could finish her thought. "How's my favorite sister?" He bent and gave Dani a kiss on the cheek as he presented the flowers with a flourish.

"I'm your only sister and I'm fine." She returned his kiss and took the flowers. "These are lovely, Shamus."

"My pleasure. And how are you, Rebecca?" He gave her a quick peck on the cheek as well.

Rebecca smiled at Shamus. It was impossible not to smile at him. He was young, good-looking and full of mischief. "I'm fine and I really must be going." She stood and gathered up her purse.

"Not on my account, I hope." Taking off his jacket, he tossed it across the end of the bed.

"No, I've got to be getting home. Jake and Casey are waiting for me." It was the truth, just not quite the way it sounded. "You take care and I'll call you in a couple of days." She bent to give Dani a hug as she spoke. "I'll be seeing you," she added to Shamus as she left the room with a wave goodbye. If she continued to live above Greer's, she probably would see more of Shamus.

She took the elevator down to the lobby and exited the hospital into the cool night air. Taking a deep breath to rid her nostrils of the antiseptic smell, she turned to walk home.

It was still early and she suddenly realized that she didn't want to go home and face Jake. Not yet. She thought about going to a movie, but decided against it. She didn't want to sit in the darkness of the theater and think about the many times that she and Jake had gone to see a movie. Everywhere she went there were memories of Jake.

She hadn't gone more than a block when a horn blew beside her, making her jump. She spun around and there was Jake rolling down the window of his truck.

"Want to go for an ice cream?"

"An ice cream?" She wasn't sure she'd heard him properly.

"Sure. Casey and I decided we wanted an ice cream. Didn't we, Casey?" Jake spoke to the little girl strapped into the seat next to him.

She nodded her head vigorously. "Come for ice cream, Aunt Rebecca."

Rebecca could not ignore the plea in Casey's eyes. For a moment, she thought she saw a similar expression in Jake's eyes, but then it was gone. She was only seeing what she wanted to see.

If she was truthful with herself, she wanted to go with them. For just a little while longer, she wanted things to seem normal. "I'd like that." She climbed into the passenger side and buckled her seat belt.

The smile Jake gave her was so gentle it made her heart beat faster. Flustered, she turned away, fiddling unnecessarily with her seat belt. By the time she looked back again, Jake had turned away and was heading the truck towards the downtown area and the promised ice cream.

Chapter Nineteen

Rebecca stood before him in a gown of shimmering white, her smile soft and gentle as she beckoned to him. Small and slender, she appeared almost fairy-like with her pale skin and enormous blue eyes. He reached out to her, almost afraid to touch her, but needing her more than he needed his next breath. As he was about to touch her face, she vanished.

In a panic, he called her name. Running through the orchards, he called to her, over and over again. He couldn't lose her. He just couldn't.

Catching a glimpse of white in the distance, he ran harder. He ran until his heart felt like it would explode. His breath was labored, his stomach clenched in fear, but still he ran. If he stopped he would lose her forever. He ran and he ran...

The sound of his own rough voice calling her name woke him. He lay there gasping for breath, sweat rolling down his forehead. Rubbing his hands over his face, he slowly sat up in bed.

"What a nightmare." But that's all it was, he reassured himself. *Just a dream.*

There was no way he would allow that dream to come true. If all went as planned, Rebecca would be home with him by the end of the day. Thinking about that made him feel better, though slightly nervous. It was still possible, even likely, that she would spurn him one final time. It was a chance he was willing to take. He had no choice.

He stretched his lean, muscled body and pulled himself out of bed. Heading to the shower, he made a mental list of what he had left to do before he met Rebecca this afternoon. The first item on his to-do-list, right after he showered, shaved and dressed, was to call on Rebecca and ask her and Casey to have supper with him tonight. He knew she wouldn't refuse if Casey was involved.

It had been hard to take them back to Rebecca's old apartment last night. He'd never considered eating ice cream to be an erotic experience before, but after his experience yesterday, it was high on his list. Just watching Rebecca consume her chocolate-covered sundae, the way she moaned in delight, the way she closed her eyes, and the way she licked the chocolate from the spoon had made him hard.

Turning the water on cold, he stepped into the shower. If he didn't get his wife home soon he'd be a wreck. He lathered the soap over his body, scrubbed, rinsed quickly and climbed out of the shower. Wrapping a towel around his waist, he stared at himself in the bathroom mirror. Running his hand over his chin, he decided he'd shave now and save time later.

Twenty minutes later, he hurried down the stairs to the kitchen. He grabbed his leather jacket on the way out the back door. First, he'd go see Rebecca and then he'd head to Jessie's for a final planning session and breakfast.

As he rapped on Rebecca's front door, Jake heard voices inside. One low and soft, the other higher pitched and excited. Before he had a chance to knock again, the door flew open.

"Uncle Jake! Uncle Jake!" Casey threw her arms around him. "I missed you."

Picking her up, he hugged her tight as he carried her into the kitchen. "I missed you too, honey."

"When can we go home? I miss my bedroom."

Jake spoke without thinking. "You can go home later today and you'll be tucked in your own little bed tonight." He kissed Casey's dark curls.

His head snapped up when he heard a gasp. Rebecca stood there as white as a ghost. He put Casey down and started towards her. "Are you all right?"

She nodded, but he ignored her easy dismissal of his concern. She was much too pale for his liking. He took her by the arm and led her to one of the kitchen chairs, not letting go of her until she was seated. "Take a deep breath."

"I'm fine, just a little dizzy." When he looked concerned she added, "I haven't been sleeping well." Taking her at her word, he nodded.

"You need to take better care of yourself, sweetheart, or you'll get sick." He reached into the cupboard for a glass and rummaged around inside the refrigerator until he found some orange juice. He poured her a glass and handed it to her. "Drink up."

When she made no move to drink it, he tipped the bottom of the glass with his finger. It was either drink it or wear it, so she drank it. He had to admit, she looked better after she finished it.

Rebecca took a deep breath before she spoke. "What time do you want to pick up Casey?"

Jake was still a little concerned about Rebecca's coloring. She was way too pale, but he supposed it was understandable if she was sleeping no better than he was. "Actually, I'd like to pick the two of you up at about four-thirty and take you out to an early supper." He watched her facial expression carefully for a sign of hesitation or rejection.

Casey squealed with excitement. "Where are we going?"

Jake reached down and tousled the child's hair. "I think I'd like to take you two out to Jessie's for supper. If that's okay with you?" he added, with a glance toward his wife.

"That would be fine." Her voice was quiet, her face averted. "Was there any particular reason you wanted to go out?"

"No reason. At least nothing I'd like to get into now." He figured she was quiet because she was tired. "Why don't you try and get a little nap after lunch. It'll make you feel better."

Leaning down, he kissed Casey and gave her a quick hug. "I'll see you later. You be a good girl for your aunt."

"I will," she promised.

Reaching out to Rebecca, he gave her a quick kiss on the cheek. "You be a good girl too and take that nap. We'll talk tonight." Closing the door behind him, he made his way down over the stairs. He couldn't wait to see her face later today when he surprised her.

Rebecca was running late. She sat down on the bed and smoothed her last pair of pantyhose up the full length of her legs. Her first two pairs had runs in them, due to her haste, and now both sat discarded on the floor. She couldn't afford to ruin her last pair.

When she had her pantyhose on, she glanced at her watch. Jake would be here any minute. Why did this kind of thing always happen when she was in a hurry? Her doctor's appointment had run way over time, but it had been worth it.

Doctor Parker had confirmed that she was pregnant, healthy, and would deliver in about six months. She had several prescriptions for prenatal vitamins and a list of instructions to follow. What she didn't have was anyone to share it with.

Rebecca sat there trying to gather her wits. This morning's conversation with Jake played over and over in her mind. Casey was going home with him today, and he hadn't said one word about her going with them. He had asked her once and it seemed he wasn't going to ask her again. She had gambled and lost. She could think of only one reason for this meeting. If Jake was taking Casey home, he must have separation papers for her to sign already.

Swiping at the tears in her eyes, she got up from the bed and took a deep breath to pull herself together. She opened the closet and shuffled through her few dresses. Pulling out her favorite one, she tugged it over her head. It was a plain green velvet that fell to just below her knees and had long, fitted sleeves. Jake had seen it many times before but she always felt pretty and confident in this dress. For tonight's supper she figured she needed all the help she could get.

She hurried and sprayed a little perfume behind her ears and on her pulse points. When she was finished, she stood back and gazed at herself in the mirror. She looked good. She knew she was no raving beauty, but she wanted to look her best. The last thing she wanted was Jake's pity.

She was slipping into her shoes and checking her purse to make sure she had everything she needed when a knock came on the door. Her stomach felt as if it had a million butterflies dancing inside. Taking one final deep breath, she abandoned the safety of the bedroom and headed for the kitchen.

When she opened the door, she nearly stopped breathing altogether. Jake was beautiful. She knew he would have scoffed at her description, but to her, he was beautiful. He was wearing a black suit, which conformed perfectly to his body and showcased his incredibly broad shoulders. His shirt was as white as snow. The only color at all was a green tie, which matched his eyes perfectly.

"Can I come in?" His voice was a husky whisper.

She stepped back from the door to let him in, and he didn't take his eyes off her as he stepped into the apartment. Talking was beyond her and they stood there for an awkward moment simply staring at each other. Lucky for her, Casey came running out from the living room.

"Look at me, Uncle Jake. I'm all dressed up." She spun around, giving him a good look at her.

"So you are and you look very pretty too." He looked Casey over carefully and then glanced at Rebecca. His eyes were hot as they looked her up and down. "You both do."

Flustered, Rebecca made a show of putting her coat on before helping Casey into hers. When she looked up, Jake was smiling at her. "We're ready."

"So you are." He waited while Rebecca locked the door before taking both their hands and helping them down the stairs and into the truck.

"You can pick up Casey's things after supper. They're all packed."

"Hmm," was all Jake would reply.

Rebecca sat there in silence as they drove to Jessie's Diner, clenching her purse in her hands. The bouncing of the truck, coupled with her emotions, was making her stomach slightly sick. She was glad Casey was there to fill in the silence as she chattered to Jake about what she'd done all day. Rebecca's heart leapt when Casey told him that they'd been to the doctor's office.

"Just a check-up," she added hastily before Jake could question her too closely. She wasn't really lying, she told herself. It was a check-up. Of sorts.

Jake and Casey continued to talk while she sat there in silence, staring at the green glow of the dashboard lights. She didn't know if she could get through this evening without breaking down and begging Jake to take her home with him. She was so lost in thought that she jumped when Jake opened her door. Glancing at the familiar sign in front of her, she realized they were parked in front of the diner.

"Right this way." Jake took her gently by the arm and led her towards the door. If she didn't know better she'd have thought he sounded nervous. But what did he have to be nervous about? Now she was projecting her own feelings onto him.

Casey ran on ahead and was already inside when Rebecca strolled into the diner in front of Jake. She came to an abrupt stop just inside the door. There looked to be a private party here tonight. The place was decorated in ribbons and flowers, and the tables were set with fancy tablecloths and candles. Sitting on the counter was a beautiful wedding cake. Someone was getting married. She had to get out of here. She couldn't take this. Biting her lip hard to keep from crying, she turned to the silent man at her side.

"We have to leave." Her voice sounded desperate, but she didn't care. Suddenly, she noticed the quiet. A dish clattered, sounding as loud as a cannon shot. Rebecca turned to find everyone there was staring at her. Still, nobody spoke. She knew everyone, but she didn't have a clue who was getting married.

"Rebecca."

She turned and faced Jake when he said her name, and was shocked by the tender look in his eyes.

Bending slowly down on one knee, his hand shook slightly as he took her hand in his. He cleared his throat. "Will you marry me?"

She thought she was going mad. She shook her head to clear her hearing. "Marry you?"

"Yes, marry me." Jake was still on bended knee in front of her. The look in his eyes was almost bleak as his hand tightened around hers.

"But, Jake," she whispered. "We're already married." She tugged on her hand, glancing nervously at the crowd avidly watching them.

Jake smiled at the confusion in her eyes. "We didn't do it right the first time. You deserve more than a quick ceremony in a judge's office."

Her heart pounded simultaneously with both excitement and dread. Everything she wanted was being handed to her, but she couldn't take it until she knew for sure. "Why?"

Jake was no longer smiling as he stood and loomed almost menacingly above her. "Why?"

"Yes, why do you want to marry me?" The expression on his face should have been frightening, but she knew in her heart she didn't have to fear his temper.

"Because I love you, damn it!" he yelled. "Do you think I'd go through another wedding if I didn't have to?" Jake flushed and looked around when he heard a few laughs from the people behind them.

"We're getting married and that's that." His voice was low and hard, but his hands were gentle as he took her face in his hands and added softly, "I can't live without you."

Rebecca couldn't believe her ears. Jake loved her. He honestly, truly loved her. In front of all their friends, he had declared himself. She flung herself into his strong arms, which wrapped themselves around her and held her tight. "I love you too."

A cheer went up from behind them, but she hardly heard it. She had eyes only for Jake. He hugged her so tight she could barely breathe, but she didn't care. It was heaven to be back in his arms.

Pulling away, he reached into his pocket and drew out a small blue velvet box. "This is for you." Jake opened the box and drew out the ring nestled inside. "If you don't like it we can exchange it for something else."

Rebecca looked down at the ring he held between his fingers. It was a diamond set inside a heart. He thrust it towards her as an offering. "Oh, Jake, it's beautiful." She held out her hand and he slipped it onto her finger. Her fingers automatically closed into a fist. She was never taking it off. Jake reverently lifted her closed hand to his lips and kissed it gently.

She tried. She really did. But she couldn't stop the tears from falling. This was how she had dreamed it should be. Jake had made her dreams come true.

"Enough of that. We've got a wedding to perform." Jessie stepped up to the couple and hugged first Jake and then Rebecca. "Come on, Rebecca, you've got to get changed."

She looked quizzically at Jessie. "Changed?"

"Yep, that husband of yours bought you a dress. Casey, too."

Rebecca was quickly hustled into the kitchen area where Jessie helped her and Casey change into their dresses. She ran her hand over the smooth white silk. It was absolutely perfect. The dress fit her as if it had been made especially for her. The hem fell below her knees and had a sweetheart neckline. White flowers were embroidered along the neckline and around the cuffs of the long sleeves.

Jake had even thought of flowers. She had a beautiful bouquet of pink roses to carry and, rather than wear a veil, she had Jessie help her pin one of the flowers in her hair.

Rebecca dabbed at the tears that threatened her newly reapplied mascara. "He's thought of everything, hasn't he?" It still shocked her that Jake would do something of this magnitude to show her how much he cared.

"I think he has. Lord knows he tried." Jessie turned to Casey, who was picking at her new dress of green velvet. "If you're ready, we'll go out and wait for the music." Jessie hugged them both once more and then led Casey away.

Jake was nervous. After all he'd been through, he hadn't expected this. They were already married for heaven's sake. In his heart he knew this was different. Jessie led Casey to a seat at the front, and he tugged on his coat sleeves and straightened his tie, yet again.

When someone turned on the taped music, he stopped fidgeting. Everyone had risen, and there in the doorway of the kitchen stood Rebecca. She had been beautiful before, but now she was breathtaking. She looked like an angel. He swallowed hard, overwhelmed by the fact that this beautiful, generous, giving woman loved him enough to marry him twice. He would take good care of her, forever.

Suddenly she was by his side and he was taking her hand in his. They faced Reverend Morris, a man they'd both know all their lives, as he began the ceremony. It felt right this time. Sacred. Jake repeated his vows with a full heart, knowing that this was for forever and this was the right woman.

It was almost like a dream to Rebecca. Only Jake's hold on her hand kept her anchored. She expected to float away any minute or have someone wake her up and tell her she was only dreaming. But this was no dream. Jake stood tall and proud next to her as she repeated her vows, and then the minister was pronouncing them man and wife.

"Ladies and gentlemen, may I present Mr. and Mrs. Jake Tanner," Reverend Morris said as he closed his prayer book.

They turned as one to face their friends who were all smiling and clapping. One at a time, they all stepped forward to congratulate the couple. Rebecca looked quickly for Casey and relaxed when she saw her in Jessie's arms, eating a cookie.

Burke and Dani were the first to offer congratulations. They apologized for having to leave quickly, but Dani was barely out of hospital and they didn't want to leave Shane for long.

After that came a parade of well-wishers, including Shamus, Mr. and Mrs. Greer, Sheriff Tucker and his wife Emma, Mike Sampson and his wife Katie, and many more friends and neighbors. Everyone wanted to congratulate the couple.

It was a while before they finally sat down to eat at a table with Casey and Jessie. Jessie had outdone herself, serving a cold plate with three kinds of salad and juicy slices of chicken and roast beef. Rebecca struggled to take in everything. She wanted to remember every detail of this day.

When Jake leaned over and planted a quick kiss on her lip, she laughed out loud. She was filled with such happiness, she thought she would burst. Her family was complete. Well, almost complete. She had her own surprise to tell Jake later.

They cut the cake for dessert, and while everyone was enjoying a slice and a cup of coffee, Rebecca opened wedding presents. Casey helped by handing her each present she was to open.

She was both surprised and touched by the presents. She opened one package with new flannel bed sheets, which caused a few ribald comments about her not needing them in order to be warm anymore now that she had Jake. She felt the hot blush climb her cheeks and everyone laughed.

Another package contained a tablecloth, hand embroidered with buttercups and daisies. Yet another, a silver serving tray to be used on special occasions. Through it all Jake sat next to her, touching her arm frequently, and admiring the presents as she passed them to him. His eyes rarely left her, and she felt special and loved.

This was what she had missed in their first hurried wedding. Tonight she felt like a bride. All dressed up and sharing the moment with friends. After the last present was opened, Rebecca stood and addressed everyone there.

"I want to thank you all for the wonderful presents. I'll cherish them forever, but I most especially want to thank you for being here today. It means a lot to me that you would all be here on such short notice to surprise me and to help Jake." Rebecca raised her glass and toasted her friends.

Jake picked up his wineglass as he stood beside her. She watched him, filled with pride, as he spoke. "Thank you, from the bottom of my heart, for helping to make this moment happen." He turned to her and raised his glass. "To my wife Rebecca. How did I ever get this lucky?"

Blushing with pleasure, she kissed him. As she pulled away, she whispered in his ear. "We're both lucky."

Jake smiled as he kissed her again.

Chapter Twenty

"She's finally asleep."

Jake turned as she stepped onto the back porch to join him, letting the door swing shut behind her. Reaching out for her, he settled her in his arms. "That's good."

"She was worn out by all the excitement, but she didn't want to go to sleep. I think she was afraid she might miss something." Rebecca snuggled close.

"She certainly seemed to enjoy herself." He chuckled and shook his head. "All that sugar didn't help her much either. She even had cake and icing in her hair."

Rebecca loved to hear Jake laugh. She relaxed in his arms, feeling her back against his solid chest, his arms wrapped around hers and his hands clasped over hers. It was a beautiful night. The stars were out and the air was crisp. The moon was a solid glowing orb as it illuminated the trees in the orchard beyond the yard. She should be cold, but in Jake's arms she was warm. It was a warmth that came from deep in her soul and had more to do with love than the temperature. His sheltering arms provided warmth in more ways than one. She was content to just stand here all night with him.

He rubbed her hair with his cheek, as if wanting even more contact with her. "I think it's time for our wedding night," he whispered in her ear.

When she tried to move out of his embrace, his arms tightened around her. Before she could move, he scooped her up and held her tight against his chest. Her arms draped around his neck as her head nestled closer to the steady beat of his heart.

"It's tradition for the groom to carry the bride over the threshold." He nudged the door open with his shoulder. "Welcome home, Mrs. Tanner," he murmured as he lowered his mouth to hers. It was a sweet kiss, full of love and tenderness.

He lowered her long enough to lock the door and then scooped her up again and headed for the stairs. As he climbed the stairs with her in his arms, she counted her blessings. Her life was full and complete.

When they reached the bedroom, Jake let her down slowly. Her body glided over his until her feet touched the floor. Her arms remained twined around his neck as she refused to relinquish contact with him for even a second. Standing on her tiptoes, she gently pulled his head down to meet hers.

"Love me, Jake," she whispered in a voice gone husky with passion.

"I do, sweetheart, and I will," he promised.

Their lips met in a kiss and this one, while not soft and sweet, was full of love. It spoke of a passion long denied and of need, on both their parts. He moved her backward until they were standing next to the bed, never breaking contact with her lips for even a moment.

Jake kissed his way down the side of her neck. All the while his hands roamed all over her body. He touched her everywhere, as if he couldn't get enough of her.

Rebecca could barely breathe, but who needed to breathe anyway. Her entire being was filled with Jake. She released her hold on his neck, running her hands down over the broad plane of his back. From there she moved to his waist and up his hard muscled chest. When he groaned she smiled. It was only fair that she could make him moan, because he was turning her insides to melted butter.

He pulled away and tugged his shirt open. Buttons flew everywhere, but neither of them cared. She needed to feel his bare skin under her hands.

Rebecca ran her fingers over his bronzed skin. All the years of working in the sun had left it light brown even after a long winter. She loved the feel of the crisp hair that covered his chest. As she grazed his nipples with her fingertips, he moaned again.

"Lady, you're playing with fire."

"I certainly hope so."

Jake reached behind her and found the zipper in her dress. He pulled it down quickly and skimmed the material down her body in two seconds flat. As the silk pooled at her feet, he stared at her. She stood there clad only in her underwear.

Impatient now, he tugged her panty hose down her legs and shrugged when he heard them rip. "I'll buy you another pair," he promised as he gently lifted each foot and eased them from her, tugging her shoes off at the same time.

"That's okay, I've got plenty more." She happily lied as she rubbed herself against him in a provocative motion. Who cared about panty hose at a time like this?

Jake lifted her against him and fell backwards onto the bed. He rolled with her until she was beneath him and then proceeded to kiss her senseless.

Her bra and panties seem to melt away at Jake's touch. She needed to be close to him, wanted his love to warm her forever. Shoving his shirt down over his shoulders, she tugged it off before reaching for the button on his pants.

Jake reared back in bed and yanked off his socks and shoes. His pants and underwear quickly followed. He reached out, pulling her back into his arms. Skin to skin, with nothing between them. For a moment, he simply held her there and she reveled in the sensation.

Rebecca burrowed closer to Jake. She wanted to absorb him into her. She lifted her hips to invite him in and he quickly filled her. They wanted each other too much to delay any longer.

They moved together, finding a rhythm, a dance that was all their own, and when they reached the stars they reached them together.

Jake lay face down on the bed, gasping for breath. She'd be the death of him, but what a way to go. He knew he must be crushing her. Somehow he found the strength to roll off her and pull her into his arms.

"How did I ever live without you?" He hardly recognized the raspy sound of his own voice.

"You'll never be without me again," she promised, gently stroking his arm. "Jake, do you want to have children?" She broached the subject cautiously.

Jake stretched a little and pulled her more securely into his arms. Her short hair tickled his chin making him smile. The image of her carrying his child filled his brain, and he liked the picture more than he'd ever imagined he could. He'd all but given up on the idea of having children of his own. "Yeah, I'd like children." Maybe a tiny pixie-like girl with short brown hair and big blue eyes like her mother. Or perhaps a son with dark hair and green eyes. If he was truly blessed, maybe they'd have one of each. Either way he loved the idea.

"Soon?"

"Sure, I don't see any reason to wait if you don't want to. You may even be pregnant now. We didn't use any protection." He found the prospect appealing.

"How about in six months or so?"

"Honey, it takes nine months." He chuckled and squeezed her tight. When she didn't reply, his brain that had been fogged with passion and sleep suddenly kicked in. "You're pregnant!"

He reared up in bed so quickly Rebecca fell out of his arms. "Yes, I am." She watched him closely, an expectant look in her eyes. Her hands tugged nervously at the bed sheets.

He stared at her, his mouth hanging open. "Pregnant." He had to say it again to believe it.

Rebecca nodded.

Tearing the covers from her body, he exposed her body to his view. Cautiously, he covered her belly with his hand. He couldn't believe his child was nestled safe inside her. "Are you okay? You need to see a doctor?" She was going to have his child. He couldn't take his eyes off her still flat stomach.

"I'm okay. I saw the doctor earlier today."

Jake's head snapped up and his voice was deadly quiet. "You knew you were pregnant when you left me," he accused.

"Yes."

Pain knifed through him. How could she have left him when she was carrying his child? He hadn't realized he'd asked the question out loud until she answered him.

"I would never have kept your child from you, Jake. I knew you'd love the baby, but I couldn't trap you in an unhappy marriage." Her eyes filled with tears and she swallowed hard. "I didn't mean to hurt you. I love you too much."

He saw her tears and felt his own eyes burn. The sincerity in her voice and on her face was all too real. He was amazed by the enormity of the love this woman had for him.

"Listen to me." He gently cupped her face with his hands. They were large hands. Callused hands. But they touched her with a gentleness that came easy to him where she was concerned. "I love you, and I love the baby, and you'll never doubt it again."

"No," she firmly agreed. "I'll never doubt it again."

Pulling her back into his arms again, he ran his hand over her belly. It was a miracle. "We're having a baby."

Laughing at the amazement in his voice, she reassured him. "Yes, we are. Do you want a boy or a girl?"

"I don't care as long as it's healthy." His earlier thoughts popped back in his head and he revised his answer. "Maybe one of each."

"As long as it's not at the same time, I'm game."

He planted a quick kiss on her lips. It was wonderful to be able to share this moment with her. To lie here together and talk about the baby made the whole thing seem more real.

Jake jerked up in bed again. "This morning you were sick. It was from the baby, wasn't it?" He glared accusingly at her.

"I'm fine, Jake." She tried to pull him into her arms, but he resisted. "A little too much stress and some morning sickness, but the doctor assures me I'm perfectly healthy."

"I want to talk to your doctor tomorrow." Somebody needed to take care of her. She worked too hard and didn't seem to understand that she was a delicate little thing. As her husband it was his duty to take care of her.

"If you want to. But honestly, Jake, I'm as healthy as a horse."

Nope, she didn't understand how delicate she was, but that was okay. She had him to take care of these kinds of things now. Sighing out loud, he lay back down again and settled her in his arms. He'd make sure she didn't do too much in the next few months. She was far too important to him to take any chances with.

Once more during the night they made love. This time it was gentle and slow as he took the time to explore the changes in his wife's body. They were subtle, but they were there. Her breasts were slightly larger and very tender. He also discovered that while her stomach was still flat, it was now harder than it had been before. He fell asleep with her in his arms and more content then he'd ever been in his entire life.

When he awoke the next morning, she was still wrapped tightly in his arms. He lay there and watched the sunlight stream through the window and settle on them. He didn't recognize the feeling filling him at first, because it was one he'd felt so rarely in his life. He was happy.

His life had changed dramatically in the last few months. Gone were the days of loneliness. Ahead he saw days filled with love and with a family. They would have good times and bad times, but they would always have each other and that would make the difference. He could get through anything with this woman at his side.

Rebecca stirred in his arms. She nuzzled his neck as she slowly stretched. She wrapped her arms around his neck and hugged him. Life didn't get any better than this.

"Good morning. How do you feel?" He worried last night might have been too much for her. He'd have to be extra careful with her while she was pregnant and not tire her too much.

"I feel wonderful, but I could feel better," she added.

"What can I do for you, sweetheart?" He pushed her hair away from her face and dropped a kiss on her forehead.

"You can love your wife." She gave him a sultry smile and then kissed him. It was a long, lingering kiss.

"With pleasure," he replied and then proceeded to do just that.

Epilogue

Rebecca walked up the stairs, holding the rail tightly. It was hard to get around now that she resembled a beach ball with legs. Making her way into the workshop, she stopped and watched Jake work. He was so intent on his carving that he hadn't heard her yet. She loved to watch him while he worked on his creations. She was still overcome with her love for this man and still awed by his love for her.

Her stomach tightened as another contraction hit and she bit back a moan. She didn't have time to wait any longer.

"Jake, it's time."

"In a minute, honey, I want to finish this piece before bed." Jake kept working on the carving in front of him.

Rebecca almost laughed at the absurdity of it all. "Jake, it's *time*." She spoke a little more sharply this time.

"In a second."

She opened her mouth to speak again, but all that came out was a groan of pain as another contraction hit her. If Jake didn't take her to the hospital soon, she'd be having the baby at home.

Jake's head jerked up when he heard the sound of pain Rebecca made. Immediately he jumped from his seat and rushed to her side. "What's wrong, honey?" She could sense his panic as he wrapped his arms around her. "Talk to me, honey," Jake pleaded.

"It is time. Now!" She enunciated each word carefully so there would be no doubt.

Jake jerked back, like he'd been slugged in the stomach with a two by four. "It can't be time. It's too early. I've got two weeks."

Rebecca laughed. She couldn't help herself. "You may have two weeks, but the baby is coming now."

Jake swung her up into his arms and started carefully down the stairs, pausing only long enough to close the door behind him. "Why didn't you say so sooner?"

Rebecca burst into fresh peals of laughter. This was too much. "I did try," she managed to gasp out in between laughs.

"Think I'm funny, do you?" He held her tight and gave her a mock glare.

Rebecca's laugh turned to a moan of pain as another contraction hit, this one a little stronger than the last.

Now he really looked worried. He strode to the truck and managed to open the door and tuck her inside. He ran around to the driver's side and climbed in.

"Jake."

"Hold on, honey, and I'll get you to the hospital in no time." He reached out to start the truck and suddenly realized he didn't have his keys.

"Jake."

Her voice was sharp enough that he finally glanced over at her. She smiled at him, her face filled with such love that he reached out and pulled her into his arms. "You'll be all right, love, I'll be with you," he promised.

"I know I'll be fine, but you've got to go get Casey. I left her getting dressed and my suitcase is at the bottom of the stairs. I already called Jessie, so she's expecting us to drop Casey off at her place on the way to the hospital." She paused for a breath. "Oh, and your coat and car keys are on the chair in the kitchen."

Jake seemed momentarily stunned. Then chagrined. "You've got it all under control. Do you need me for anything?" he joked.

Rebecca replied very seriously. "I need you more than I need air to breathe. I need you for everything." And as another contraction hit, she added truthfully, "I also need you to drive me to hospital."

Jake sprinted into the house and grabbed his coat and keys on his way to the bottom of the stairs. Casey was sitting patiently next to Rebecca's suitcase.

"Is Mom okay, Dad?" she asked in a small voice.

A thrill went through Jake. He didn't think he'd ever get used to her calling him Dad. It felt good. They'd never wavered in their decision to adopt Casey. When they'd asked her how she felt about being adopted, she had cried. He'd sat there, helpless in the face of her tears, until she had asked him if that would make him her new dad. When he had nodded, she'd flung her little arms around him and said that she wanted them to be her dad and mom more than anything else in the entire world. Both he and Rebecca had cried that night as well.

He stooped down and picked her up in his arms. "Mom's gonna be fine and in a few hours you'll be a big sister." He tweaked her on the nose. "What do you think of that?"

"Okay," she replied and snuggled into his shoulder and yawned.

Jake carried her and the suitcase out to the truck and loaded both aboard. He headed to town, stopping only long enough to deposit Casey at Jessie's house. They had discussed this with Casey, so she was expecting to stay with Jessie and was looking forward to the games Jessie had promised to play with her.

Their arrival at the hospital was a blur. He stopped the truck at the emergency entrance, lifted Rebecca out of the vehicle and hurried inside. A nurse quickly appeared and, taking in the situation with an experienced glance, directed him to put Rebecca in a wheelchair. He didn't want to let her go, but forced himself to gently place her in the chair. She cried out in pain, panting to gain control. The nurse took over and whisked her away. He started to follow, but was stopped by another nurse.

"Mr. Tanner, you have to move your truck." She gave him an encouraging pat on the shoulder. "By the time you do that and get the paperwork done, your wife will be all prepped and waiting for you."

He didn't think he'd ever moved as fast in his life. He parked in the first available slot and raced back inside. There was so much activity, things to be done, forms to be signed. He was exhausted by the time he finally made it to the delivery room. Then came the long night of labor. Jake didn't know how he made it.

Samuel Jacob Tanner came into the world just before breakfast on the second day of November. He was two weeks early, but strong, healthy, and eager to face the world.

Jake stared at the child in his arms, unable to believe the little bundle was his son. He was tiny, yet perfect. It was hard to imagine such a small creature causing such an uproar.

Remembering how he reacted when Rebecca had come out to his workshop to tell him it was time, he laughed at himself. "Daddy wasn't a whole lot of help at first," he told the child in his arms.

He laughed again and looked down at his sleeping son. "Mommy did all the work, but Daddy is sure beat out."

"Jake." Rebecca opened her eyes and gazed sleepily up at him. "He's perfect, isn't he." It was a statement, not a question.

"Absolutely," he agreed. "As perfect as his mother." Jake carefully tucked his son into Rebecca's waiting arms. Her brown hair was sticking up in short spikes, and there were shadows under her blue eyes, but she had never looked as beautiful to him as she did at this moment. He pulled the bedcovers over her and tucked them around her.

"Thank you for making my life complete and for giving me a family." He gently smoothed her hair away from her face as he bent down to kiss her softly on the lips. "I love you, Rebecca."

She looked at him with all the love she felt for him shining from her eyes. "You're very welcome. It's only fair since you've done the same for me."

Unable to resist, Jake eased himself down on the bed and gathered both mother and child in his arms. By the time the nurse came to take the baby back to the nursery, they were all sound asleep.

N.J. Walters

N.J. Walters has always been a voracious reader of romance novels and decided one day that she could write one as well. The contemporary story, *Discovering Dani*, was the very first novel she wrote while living in a little town much like the one Dani O'Rourke lives in, though all other similarities to Dani's life pretty much end there. Then she wrote another one that followed up on Dani's friends and neighbors. But she didn't consider herself a "real" writer yet.

Just a few years later N. J. had a mid-life crisis at a fairly young age, gave notice after ten years at her job on a Friday and received a tentative acceptance for her first published novel (an erotic romance) from a publisher on the following Sunday.

Happily married for over eighteen years to the love of her life, with his encouragement and support she gave up the job of selling books for the more pleasurable job of writing them. She now spends her days writing, reading and reviewing books. It's a tough life, but someone's got to do it. And some days she actually feels like a "real" writer.

N.J. enjoys hearing from readers, and she can be reached at njwalters22@yahoo.ca. You can check out her web site at www.njwalters.com.

Also by N. J. Walters

Discovering Dani available in ebook and print!

Discovering Dani
by N.J. Walters
Available from www.SamhainPublishing.com

Burke Black wanted something he could live with, but ended up finding someone he could live for. Book 1 of Jamesville.

Dani O'Rourke has had the responsibility of raising her two brothers, Patrick and Shamus, since the death of their parents. As sole owner and operator of O'Rourke Cleaning Services, she is no stranger too hard work, but she is a beginner when it comes to men.

Burke is a very rich and successful businessman whose brush with death has made him question his priorities. He's traveled to Jamesville for peace and quiet while he plans the rest of his life.

Their lives collide when Burke accuses her of breaking into his cabin to steal from him. Their attraction to each other is immediate, and after a series of misunderstandings he finds himself caught up in the lives of Dani and her brothers.

But can this gentle, giving woman get a man as hard and cynical as Burke to believe in the power of love? Or will Burke leave town without ever discovering the wonders of life with Dani?

Enjoy the following excerpt of *Discovering Dani*

"Don't just stand there, man, push!"

Dani O'Rourke flinched inwardly even as she stepped up to the beige Mercedes and placed her mitten-covered hands next to a large pair of leather-gloved hands on the cold, hard bumper. She shoved as hard as she could, while the car's wheels spun crazily in the slush.

"Harder!" the male voice growled.

Bracing her booted feet as best she could on the snow-covered ice, Dani pushed with all her might.

"Again!" the voice demanded. Once more, she threw her weight against the back of the car as it started to rock back and forth.

"Put some muscle into it," the male voice ordered.

One more shove sent the car spinning from the icy patch and a shower of cold snow spraying into her face. Dani sputtered and swiped at her face with her black wool mitten as she straightened up and watched the man who had issued the terse commands walk slowly toward the front of the car without a backward glance.

"Thank you ever so much," a girlish voice gushed from the driver's seat. "I don't know what I would have done if you hadn't stopped to help."

Sighing, Dani turned away and trudged down the road, unnoticed by either. She knew the car's owner, or more specifically, she knew about the car's owner. Everyone in Jamesville was familiar with Cynthia James and the James family. Her family's ancestors had settled the town a hundred years before and were still heavily involved in real estate and banking. Cynthia was beautiful and she knew it. She had the long blonde hair, blue-eyed, California girl appearance that men seemed to find irresistible. All she had to do was bat her eyelashes and smile, and men fell all over themselves to please her.

Dani pictured the stranger in her mind's eye, wondering who he was. Born and raised in Jamesville, she knew everyone, if not personally, then by sight. She suspected he was probably visiting friends or just passing through.

What does it matter to you? She scolded herself impatiently. A man like that would never notice a woman like her. Her hair was a plain medium brown that was usually worn in a no-nonsense braid that fell to her waist, and she'd never had the money or the inclination to wear makeup. Her few attempts at mascara and eyeliner had left her feeling more like a raccoon than a model. Somehow, she never felt quite right if she was wearing anything more than lip-gloss.

She could still picture his coal black hair, damp and shining from the falling snow. Eyes almost as black as his hair, snapping with impatience, as he'd issued his commands. An aura of power and arrogance had surrounded him as he'd barked his orders with no doubt that they would be followed.

Of course, she reasoned, he had the size to back it up. He was built like a mountain, tall and broad, with a face that looked as if it were carved from stone. A long jagged scar had bisected his left cheek. Dani thought it gave him the dangerous air of a pirate or a highwayman. *Just like the unsuspecting hero in a romance novel,* she mused.

"Stop it, Dani O'Rourke," she muttered as she reached her truck and dug into her pocket for her keys. "He thought you were a man, for heaven's sake." But she could understand why. At five-foot-eight, she was a tall woman and solidly built. Not overweight, but sturdy. Wearing her brother's hand-me-down parka that zipped around her face and covered her to her knees, well, it was no wonder he had mistaken her for a male. She consoled herself even as she wondered why the thought made her head hurt.

She had wasted enough time, lusting for things she could not have. There was work to do. It was the same lecture she had been scolding herself with for the past seven years, ever since her mother died and she became sole guardian of her brothers. If it sounded a little flat, well, that was just too bad, she told herself as she unlocked the door to her truck and prepared herself to face the rest of the day.

Samhain Publishing, Ltd.

It's all about the story...

Action/Adventure
Fantasy
Historical
Horror
Mainstream
Mystery/Suspense
Non-Fiction
Paranormal
Red Hots!
Romance
Science Fiction
Western
Young Adult

http://www.samhainpublishing.com

Printed in the United States
59832LVS00003B/1-144

9 781599 982526